X

5

BOOKS BY MARK ALDANOV

———

THE TENTH SYMPHONY
BEFORE THE DELUGE
FOR THEE THE BEST
THE FIFTH SEAL

———

CHARLES SCRIBNER'S SONS

THE TENTH SYMPHONY

THE
TENTH
SYMPHONY

By

MARK ALDANOV

Translated by
GREGORY GOLUBEFF

CHARLES SCRIBNER'S SONS, NEW YORK

1948

FOREWORD BY THE AUTHOR

IN ONE of the remote rooms of the Louvre, beyond the furniture section, hang Isabey's pictures. A small, oblong room with yellow-brown walls, a gray door with a gold stripe, not five times taller (like the doors in the main halls) but only twice the height of a man. The only window is covered. The room is nearly always half dark. It is not easy to examine thoroughly the small pictures in old, gilded, black and brown frames. On a small, antique table, under glass, on faded yellow velvet, lie miniatures. All this was collected and bequeathed to the Louvre by Isabey's daughter; she committed suicide fifty years ago.

These marvelous miniatures have not as yet, in my opinion, been evaluated according to their full merit. They are very diverse in character, yet in them lies an entire epoch; a genuine treasure for the historian and romantic. They give us what the huge canvases of Gros or David did not give us.

In his youth, Isabey knew people who remembered Louis XIV. The author of these pages, once in his lifetime, saw the Empress Eugénie, who

knew Isabey personally. The exciting linkage of
these eras is incomprehensible in its romance.
This perhaps is an argument in favor of the frag-
mentary art of miniatures.

Of course, *The Tenth Symphony* is by no means
an historical novel, not even a novel. According
to the design of the author it is very near to what,
in the eighteenth century, was called a philosophical novelette. To call it a symbolical novelette would be still more accurate. The fundamental symbol is quite clear: "A ladder stands
on earth and its top reaches heaven." I am afraid
that the fundamental principle is expressed too
coarsely, and the non-fundamental too impercep-
tibly. However, the reader will be the judge.

THE TENTH SYMPHONY

I

. . . e l'onor di quell'arte
Ch'alluminare e chiamata in Parisi.[1]

—DANTE

THE POLICE officer left the station hurriedly. Heavy gilded carriages were stopping at the city gate. From the general appearance of the procession the officer concluded that important persons had arrived. Probably one of the delegations, gathering from all points of Europe to attend the Congress in Vienna.

"They must be French," he thought. The carriages were such as were used in France—with low coach boxes, low front wheels and a small trunk at the rear.

A lackey, clad in a gray dust coat, jumped from the front seat of the last carriage, arranged the folding step and opened the door. A young man with a bored expression on his tired, dusty face

[1] The honor of that art which, in Paris, is called illuminating.

1

appeared. His hair, badly curled, appeared to have been powdered quite recently.

He looked around, tapped the ground with his fashionable cane, as though determining how solid the earth was, and emerged from the carriage, holding onto the door handle.

"Probably an official of the delegation, or a secretary," the officer decided, and accelerated his pace.

The young man yawned, knocked off with his cane a bit of dry mud that stuck to the carriage doorstep and, producing a paper from his pocket, eyed the approaching officer, somewhat vexed.

"*La délégation française,*" said the secretary curtly. The officer knew French. He saluted and, taking the traveling documents, offered the secretary the courtesy of proceeding without the usual formality of signing.

"Within an hour your papers will be delivered to you," he said. "You have probably arranged to stay in Prince Kannitz' palace, sir?"

The secretary did not answer. He was trying to discern through the blinding rays of the sun a newly arrived carriage.

A gentleman of middle age with a sagacious but pleasant and animated face shouted something from a distance, bending his body over the carriage door and jovially nodding his head in greeting.

"Oh, it is you, Monsieur Isabey?" inquired the secretary pleasantly, yet with condescension. "Did you sleep well?"

"Wonderfully. How could I help it after last night's supper? And you?"

"Did not shut my eyes," retorted the young man. "Yes, we shall stay at Hotel Kannitz"—this to the officer. "Not all of the delegation, naturally, but please send our papers there."

"It is very difficult now to arrange for accommodations in Vienna," said the officer with an agreeable smile. His orders were to show the arriving delegates particular attention. "Vienna is overcrowded. The Prince is already here," added the officer, displaying his knowledge of the personage who headed the French delegation.

"Yes, the greater part of the commission, with Prince Talleyrand at its head, arrived earlier. We are the last," answered the young man affably. "So within an hour you will deliver our documents?" he inquired, and proffered the officer his hand.

"You may rest assured. Good day, sir."

"Good day, Monsieur Isabey," said the secretary as he returned to his carriage. "You are on your way home—then we shall meet at dinner? The Prince usually dines at five."

"Excellent. So do I," replied Monsieur Isabey good-naturedly.

The lackey motioned to the driver of the first carriage. The officer came to salute. Monsieur Isabey arranged the cushions on the seat, moved the foot-rest and settled himself comfortably at the window.

Despite the early hour, the outskirts of the city were full of activity. Stores had opened. Inhabitants had left their houses in order to watch with curiosity the slowly moving carriages.

"Russians. No. Englishmen," they speculated among themselves.

Monsieur Isabey was smiling pleasantly. Many agreeable memories were connected with his last sojourn in Vienna, four years ago. Now, on this fresh sunny morning, he liked it even more.

"A very beautiful city and the people here are most delightful. The Emperor should never have fought with them. . . . Poor Emperor. . . . He lived for glory and he has an abundance of glory even now," mused Monsieur Isabey as he smiled sweetly at a passing little girl. She wore a short, white dress, pink slippers and a gold-laced cap. "This, I think, is the native dress. Very charming. And there is nothing in this world more beautiful

than the fresh bloom on her cheeks. What a pity
that, instead of her, I must sketch various mean,
cunning and conceited old men, whose only pleasure on this earth is to poison one another. . . .
What is he saying? To go where?"

The driver, having turned around on the coach
box, asked him something. Monsieur Isabey had
confidence in his knowledge of German. Actually,
he knew it very little.

Even before they approached the gate he explained to the driver where to go: to the suburb
Leopoldstadt, beyond the Donau Canal. Monsieur Isabey knew that in this odd tongue the
Danube was pronounced *Donau*.

"Stupid man," thought Monsieur Isabey, about
to lose his temper, but the red wrinkled face of
the old driver was pleasant and kindly. He evidently was trying hard to please the foreign guest,
and above all the sunny morning was so nice that
Monsieur Isabey did not succeed in getting angry.
After more explicit instructions the driver finally
understood.

At the canal, Monsieur Isabey ordered his
lackey to get off the coach box and take his place
on the footboard behind the carriage: it was more
seemly to approach a strange place in this manner.

Friends had already prepared an apartment
for Monsieur Isabey but arrangements had not

as yet been completed: he was to examine it personally and decide whether or not the rooms were comfortable enough and the light suitable for his work. It was impossible to depend on others for that.

The driver leaned backwards and tightened the reins. The carriage was descending towards a bridge.

"Razumovsky Brücke," said the driver.

The name was familiar to Monsieur Isabey and he recalled that a Russian count, the owner of the most gorgeous palace in Vienna, had built the bridge at his own expense. This was the most convenient way to return home from the Prater.

"A pleasant gentleman, mellowed with the wisdom of years," thought Monsieur Isabey. On his last trip to Vienna he had visited Count Razumovsky.

"What a palace and such masterpieces! And what is more surprising is his knowledge of painting. What do they call him here in Vienna? Oh, yes . . . Erzherzog Andreas?" he asked the driver with a smile. The pleased driver chuckled, nodding his head. With this achievement, the building of the bridge at his own expense, the Count evidently had exceeded the wildest fancies of the people of Vienna.

At the gate, where the carriage stopped, pleasant excitement ran high. A little girl, who sat near the gate, tore hurriedly up the stairs. Before Monsieur Isabey mounted the porch the mistress of the house came out to greet him. She was a majestic lady of middle age wearing a silk dress profusely decorated with embroidered flowers.

On the steps she had started to smile and when she reached the porch she welcomed the celebrated guest with a French salutation evidently prepared and memorized to perfection.

This welcome moved Monsieur Isabey to such an extent that he kissed her hand, thereby seriously risking the loss of her respect forever.

A wide stairway, not too steep, covered with a rather good carpet, led them upstairs. The appearance of the entrance was of great importance to Monsieur Isabey, as very distinguished people frequented his studio. The hall was quite satisfactory. A room at the end of the hall was flooded with sunshine. Monsieur Isabey sighed with delight. He had always dreamed of lighting just like this. Right there, not bothering to examine the rest of the rooms, he informed the mistress that he had decided to take the apartment and did not even bargain, despite the high price that she named. The mistress, Frau Pulvermacher, nevertheless added that any other place would cost him more, as for instance the hotel "Zum

Roemischen Kaiser." The cheapest room would cost twenty guldens a day, and even so there were no vacancies.

"Yes, I agree," repeated Monsieur Isabey.

Frau Pulvermacher nodded. She evidently liked the new tenant. She explained that her deceased husband had been an architect, then proceeded to show him the rest of the apartment, opening the doors as proof that there had been no misrepresentation on her part.

"Monsieur Issape will be satisfied." She pronounced the name of her tenant with two accents, on the first and last syllables.

True, she had not misrepresented. In the bedroom everything was in order; an enormous bed with a feather quilt, wardrobes, a washstand covered with pitchers, bowls and flagons. Monsieur Isabey's lackey, treading heavily on the steps, was carrying in the trunks and luggage. He was assisted by the chambermaid, a powerful, red-faced woman with a huge bust. "Jesus Christ be praised," she said in a hoarse voice as she entered the room.

"Lord, what a Rubens!" thought Monsieur Isabey, quite impressed.

A zinc bathtub, shaped like a shoe, was brought in. With adroitness one could sit in it. Steam emanated from the tub. Monsieur Isabey eyed the bathtub with a smile, as such an object was a rarity even in Paris. However, he did not dare sit in it.

Having washed and shaved, Monsieur Isabey, assisted by his lackey began to arrange his personal effects. He unfolded his suit of clothes, of the latest mode—narrow-waisted with silk buttons—also his hats, underwear, wigs, tobacco pouches, pistols, compass, map, and a number of other things. Everything he had was excellent. Monsieur Isabey had a weakness for expensive things. He ordered his lackey to open a large, tightly roped box: there he kept his newly started paintings, as well as the completed ones which he had brought with him for the purpose of decorating the studio.

He returned to the large room in a dark-red dressing gown with tassels. Around a large bouquet of flowers on a table, there had been placed a coffeepot, butter, tiny round rolls, ham, honey, jam, heavy silver cups and a decanter filled with liquid of a very pleasing color.

"Really, she is a fine woman. Except for that yellow dress with the roses. My God!" thought Monsieur Isabey, upon whose decree the most beautiful women in Paris waited with blind and fervent obedience.

"It is also imperative to break this porcelain

pug-dog and throw the pieces far away—" He even sighed at the thought that people should exist who fancied such things.

Monsieur Isabey drank a cup of coffee, ate a roll with butter and ham, another with butter and honey, and tried the contents of the decanter —it proved to be Tokay wine of good quality— poured himself a second cup of coffee (the coffee was both strong and delicious) and in the best of spirits went to the middle window of the room. The workshop afforded a beautiful view of the river. Over the bridge, which was divided into four lanes for carriages and pedestrians, vehicles were moving towards the Prater. Boats were glid- ing lazily along the river. Children were playing on stairways which descended in crooked lines towards the water.

The street curved to the left. Over the houses of unequal height one could see a Gothic spire in the distance.

"Oh, Lord, how wonderful!" thought Monsieur Isabey.

From the next room came sounds of hammer- ing, the splitting of boards: the lackey was open- ing the box of canvases.

"This is most important," cheerfully thought Monsieur Isabey, remembering the contents of the box. "One must work, work."

From the sun, the fresh air and the strong coffee he felt an exceptional influx of energy and, leaving the window, he began to work.

One hour later everything was in order. The pug-dog and gaudy curtains had been removed. The walls were draped with hangings and pictures brought from Paris. The easels had been placed.

Monsieur Isabey pushed a large table to the wall and there, on a plush cloth, spread his miniatures. Snuffboxes, square, round, and oval, predominated. In the center, there was a casket with the main treasure of the collection: on the lid of a small, round snuffbox, on a tiny piece of ivory, surrounded by a double circlet of gold and tiny pearls, was a portrait of the King of Rome—a beautiful child with sparkling eyes. "Nobody else could have created this," proudly thought Monsieur Isabey.

"Schoen! Sehr herzig. Très choli!" said Frau Pulvermacher in genuine ecstasy after Monsieur Isabey had invited her to share his delight in the arrangement of the studio.

She even forgave the French guest's insult— his returning with poorly concealed repulsion the porcelain pug-dog as well as the curtains which had been hung especially for him the day before.

The mistress' admiration pleased Monsieur Isabey, though he was confident that, with the exception of artists, no one understood nor was capable of understanding art. The miniature of the King of Rome met with particular success; the pearls, evidently genuine and expensive, moved her, as well as the fact that a portrait could be produced on such a tiny piece of ivory. Also that the child, though the offspring of a villain, was the grandson of her Emperor, whom she had often seen on the streets. And Monsieur Isabey had painted the portrait with the Prince posing for him in the palace, where everything was sumptuous and majestic.

Suddenly a blush covered Frau Pulvermacher's face and she informed Monsieur Isabey that there would be a change in the price of the apartment: not four hundred guldens a month, but three hundred and seventy-five. Monsieur Isabey thought at first that she had made a mistake, that she had rented her apartment too cheaply and intended raising the price. However, Frau Pulvermacher had not made a mistake. She actually reduced his rent by twenty-five guldens.

"How wonderful! This is the result of pangs of conscience. Neither Fouché nor Talleyrand has one," he said to himself. "I've always thought that they—the plain people—are the best."

II

I am sending you this message through trustworthy hands, not by mail, therefore I have taken a notion to express myself concerning your letter numbered "2", where you discuss marriage and the circumstances thereof . . . It is hardly worthwhile leaving your country forever. Even dumb animals remain near their haunts in the forest, where they were born and grew up. Still more should Man, a being endowed with a mind and intellect, adhere to this law If we reason diligently, with thoroughness, it will be found necessary to suppress every flame of passion which burns, having been kindled by blindness.

> —HETMAN KIRILL RAZUMOVSKY'S
> LETTER TO HIS SON, ANDREY

ANDREY KIRILLOVITCH RAZUMOVSKY, Erzherzog Andreas, as he was affectionately ironically called in Vienna because of his majestic carriage, strict observance of etiquette and unusually luxurious manner of living, was returning home on horseback from his daily exercise. He galloped through the upper avenue

13

of the Prater and the ride tired him. Andrey Kirillovitch was over sixty. Riding horseback was purely a matter of habit with him. His physicians had long ago advised him to discontinue this strenuous exercise, or, if he persisted, to ride slowly, on a gentle mount. Razumovsky was rather proud of the fact that he had not heeded the advice of his physicians.

At the lower Prater, as he approached the river, he stopped, removed his hat, then continued to walk his horse. He rode in the old Seidlitz style: on the shanks, with short reins, long stirrups, and on a small saddle with huge, gold-embroidered caparison. The old Holstein horse with a braided tail, biting on the bit and turning its head from side to side, caracoled, as though intending, from second to second, to take its head and throw the rider. Passing pedestrians stepped aside in admiration.

During his horseback ride Count Razumovsky had experienced a singular incident. A gentleman, mounted on a beautiful English horse, had approached him, conversed with him about the weather, then amiably taken leave. Razumovsky could not remember who he was. He did remember, however, that the gentleman was a king; but which particular king, Razumovsky failed to recall. Andrey Kirillovitch knew all the reigning

princes of Europe. At the present time a number
of them were assembled in Vienna and among
them were several kings. Daily they promenaded
or rode horseback along the Prater without attendants or aides-de-camp and even without
police guard. (In reality they were accompanied
by agents of the Vienna Secret Police but this
was accomplished without the knowledge of the
public.)

The gentleman he had met was neither the
Prussian, Bavarian, nor the Württemberg King—
he could not have failed to recognize any one of
these. "Who was he? Perhaps not a king, but an
archduke, or a prince?" he speculated. "Of Baden?
Of Weimar? Schaumburg-Lippe? Hohenzollern-
Sigmaringen? But no . . . thank goodness, these
I know well. . . . Perhaps Anton of Saxony? He
did have the appearance of living in a state of
depression," thought Andrey Kirillovitch (the
Saxons, recent allies of Napoleon, were held in
contempt by the leaders of Congress). "No, I do
remember—he *was* a king."

Razumovsky meditated on the incident with a
smile: he had addressed the gentleman as he
would have addressed a king, but avoided, with
utmost care, the use of a title, rapidly mentioning
between sentences something that sounded like a
title. The King spoke French well, though with

a slight foreign accent. This would not serve as a clue, however. "They all speak like that—very funny," thought Andrey Kirillovitch. "But his features are familiar. I am losing my memory altogether. Father's head was clear until he was eighty. No match for him!" Crossing the bridge which bore his name, he came to a street, also bearing his name, and, beyond the bend, sighted his castle. The view of the splendid edifice always afforded him pleasure. Now a heartache was mingled with this feeling. Razumovsky had decided to present the castle to his Emperor as an embassy. Society was full of rumors concerning this transaction and it had inspired many comments.

Those close to the Count knew that his affairs, far from being in a state of prosperity, would not permit him to bestow gifts worth two millions. Some ill-disposed people explained his proposed venture as a cunning diplomatic scheme; the Emperor was expected to refuse the gift but should he accept, he would undoubtedly offer Andrey Kirillovitch a permanent post as court official to the Emperor Franz. It would hardly be proper to dislodge a man from the house he had presented to the state.

Everyone knew that Razumovsky adored Vienna, had become used to it in the past twenty-five years, was married to one Austrian countess, about to marry another, and dreaded the thought of moving to another place. Others opined that Razumovsky had no such clever reason. He was just being Erzherzog Andreas, who, by nature, as a matter of course amazed people with his grandiose gestures: just as, earlier, he had bought and wrecked twenty-eight houses in order to make room for his palace—all this when he was head over heels in debt. With a similar gesture he had built at his own expense, with a view to economy, a stone bridge over the river in order to avoid the round-about way to his castle—thus saving time and therefore money. Old friends remembered with a smile how the late Hetman Kirill Grigonevitch had described in his picturesque folk language the various financial ventures of his favorite son. On the square in front of the palace (it also was named "Razumovsky") there were a few carriages. The coachmen and lackeys removed their caps in greeting. Andrey Kirillovitch nodded his head in return, at the same time examining the crests on the carriages and speculating as to whom they belonged. "What? Guests, already? So early in the day?" he thought gloomily. Not stopping at the main entrance. Razumovsky proceeded to the riding school, which had been converted into a hall for large receptions.

Here a dinner for three hundred and sixty persons was being prepared.

The Superintendent, a stout man of dignity, who was overseeing the preparations in the riding hall, noticed the Count, excitedly clapped his hands twice and, removing his high hat, quickly, with short paces, hastened towards him. The servants came running to Andrey Kirillovitch and helped him to dismount. He patted the neck of his horse, ascended the porch and, concealing his shortness of breath, glanced into the reception hall. Everything was in excellent order.

"Put on your hat. It is cold," suggested Andrey Kirillovitch in a tired voice.

The Superintendent reported on the details of the dinner preparations: the messenger, who had been sent to France after truffles, grapes and oysters, had just returned. The sturgeon from the Volga would probably arrive tomorrow. Pineapples and cherries—one could not wish for better—had also arrived. Razumovsky listened to his Superintendent not without pleasure. He rather liked the Viennese dialect. But oysters, sturgeon, and cherries were of little interest to him. He suddenly realized that the success of the dinner was of slight importance to him.

"One may suppose that the dinner will be successful for the one thousandth and first time.

Well, thank the Lord," he mused, indifferent. "However, my heart is misbehaving. . . . It's all of three minutes since I dismounted."

"But the cherries from Petersburg cost us dearly, Your Excellency—one rouble apiece, which, at the present exchange, makes them a little more than a florin," continued the worried Superintendent. "They are out of season. . . . It can't be helped. . . ."

"There's nothing you can do about it," absent-mindedly repeated Razumovsky.

"And, Your Excellency, we shall be obliged to use local butter—not one of the stores carries Danish . . ."

"Good Lord! Certainly—it was the Danish King! Of course," he discovered with relief. "But why didn't I recognize him, *ce cher* Fréderic? True, we have not met for a long time. Yet . . ."

"It can't be helped," he jokingly repeated again. "We shall use Viennese butter! Anything else?"

"No, Your Excellency. By the way, allow me to report that Herr Kapellmeister van Beethoven called and commanded me to tell Your Excellency that he cannot be present at the Palace tomorrow."

"What do you mean, he cannot be here? Why not?" exclaimed Razumovsky.

"Herr Kapellmeister did not give a reason,"

replied the Superintendent with a respectful smile. "Your Excellency knows Herr van Beethoven."

"But this is impossible! Absolutely impossible!" retorted Razumovsky, visibly annoyed. "Perhaps something has offended him."

"I would not know, Your Excellency."

"I shall write him a letter immediately," Andrey Kirillovitch said after brief thought. "By the way, do you know who is here?"

The Superintendent recited the names of the guests. At the palace of Andrey Kirillovitch the duties of hostess were assumed jointly by Countess Thurhein and her sister. The Countess was considered engaged to Andrey Kirillovitch but only unofficially. Nevertheless the Viennese ladies, who admired him, continued to visit his hospitable mansion even after the death of his first wife.

For Razumovsky, laws were violated. In fact, he himself made laws.

Having listened to the list of guests, Razumovsky knitted his brows slightly The gentlemen and ladies were all welcome but among them were two ladies of the same rank. That meant the guests would be obliged to stand all evening According to the etiquette current at that time in Vienna, a countess had to leave her seat for a princess who might enter the drawing room: she in turn would rise before a princess whose title had priority. The princesses would leave their seats for Oberhoffmeisterinnen.

Should, however, two ladies of equal rank be present, neither one could be seated and the entire company would spend the evening standing. Heretofore, the most uncomfortable formalities of etiquette had seemed reasonable and necessary to Razumovsky. Now this custom appeared to him ridiculous. "A great many things here are strange if the truth be known." Andrey Kirillovitch, slightly provoked, remembered that the Austrian Emperor shook hands only with those of his subjects who were ministers, ranked high at court, or who bore a title not less than that of count.

At receptions Razumovsky had seen Emperor Franz greet generals of long, meritorious service with only a smile and nod of his head, and in the next instant offer his hand to young titled officers.

"From various alternatives one must choose the best. We in our country are wiser and more pleasant, yet the splendor at our Emperor's receptions is no less," thought Andrey Kirillovitch. "There should be no distinction between aristocratic birth and merit. . . . What is a title? My late uncle happened to be at court at an opportune time - so we have a title. . ."

Accompanied by the Superintendent, who continued to describe various details of the morrow's dinner, Razumovsky turned to the side entrance of the palace. It was growing dark. Red leaves were falling from the trees. At the fountain Andrey Kirillovitch stopped to rest. From that place, at twilight, the palace appeared even more beautiful. "Yes, it is a pity to abandon all this forever," he thought vaguely, having in mind his proposed gift, or perhaps the other "forever."

"And at each corner, Your Excellency, we shall place escutcheons with inscriptions of the Allied Armies' victories."

A flash of light burst forth and ran along the wick. At once the windows of the two main drawing rooms and picture gallery were illuminated. With all his love for the old-fashioned order of things, Andrey Kirillovitch did not deny himself modern improvements—for example, he had installed a new system of artificial heating, the water pipes being laid under the floors, the same heating system as was installed in several salons of the Burg.

"Evidently there is no one in Canova's Hall. I shall go there, then," thought Razumovsky, as he mounted the leaf-covered stairs.

He dismissed his Superintendent. The French

valet de chambre met him at the head of the stairs.

Andrey Kirillovitch ordered him to lay out a jabot with Brabant lace, a white muslin cravat and a frock-coat. "Spider considering a crime." "How foolish it is: 'Spider considering a crime'!" he thought, surprised that the valet listened to the words as seriously as he had recited them.

Alabaster lamps were lighted in the white room, which was filled with Canova's works. One of the lamps flooded the statue of "Flora" with white light. There was a small desk at the other side of the room. Andrey Kirillovitch enjoyed working in this particular gallery.

"It is not late yet," he thought, as he looked at his watch, seated himself at the desk and began to write: "*Mein lieber Beethoven . . .*" Having written a few lines, Razumovsky fell into deep thought. He felt an increasing tiredness, his excessive heartbeat did not subside.

"Perhaps I should stop riding horseback. My late father was fond of quoting Sirach: 'Thou wert young and art grown old. A stranger shall take hold of thee and lead thee where thou would'st not go. . . . Yea, verily, where thou would'st not go.'

"The situation in the Congress is most unsatisfactory. . . . Nesselrode monopolizes everything." Razumovsky, although the ranking Russian representative, did not take an active part in the work.

"Perhaps I was appointed for the sole reason that they needed at least one Russian—the others —Nesselrode, Stäckelberg, Pozzo di Borgo, Capo d'Istrias and Anstedt . . . together they are designated as the Russian delegation in the Congress," thought Andrey Kirillovitch with irony, though he had no prejudice against aliens or foreigners. "No, there is nothing good in sight. Properly speaking, everything is gone. . . . However, in the past, success never brought me happiness. Gossip, slander, animosity, jealousy—'Behold the reverse of a mediocre medal'! My personal affairs are also uncertain. Even Horosheve[1] has been sold, after so many perturbations. All that is left is Baturin[1] and *it* is mortgaged. I have no money and Beethoven has none," thought Razumovsky, a sad smile on his face. "Only he doesn't entertain three hundred and sixty persons for dinner. He hasn't enough money to pay the shoemaker. Yet he is worth all of Vienna."

Andrey Kirillovitch reread his note, added a few polite phrases and sealed it.

[1] Razumovsky's estate in Russia.

III

What a vanity is the art of painting, which evokes admiration by a likeness to things, the originals of which one does not admire.

—PASCAL

"GENTLEMEN, one more second and you shall be at liberty. The sitting is at an end. The light has become insufficient," said Monsieur Isabey in a pleasant voice while standing with brush in hand near the easel. His sharp, half-screwed-up eyes traveled intermittently from the hall to the canvas. "Milord, lower your head a little. Thank you. Prince, your smile is delightful, but I should like to depict the Congress solemnly and seriously, as befits a gathering of such personages. Please imagine for a second that Emperor Napoleon has returned from the island of Elba. That's fine. This is wonderful!"

The delegates laughed. Even among them Monsieur Isabey was a general favorite.

"One minute more, gentlemen, just one minute. I know how valuable your time is. And today, in addition, there are the tableaux at the palace. Please don't be uneasy—you won't be late—I happen to be in charge of the production. It is at least three hours before the beginning. You will have time enough to settle even the Polish question. Monsieur President of the Congress, please favor your humble servant with a glance. Thank you! So. Gentlemen, I congratulate you—you are free. Today's sitting is over."

"Over? That's splendid."

"However, you kept us long enough."

"But progress is in evidence."

"What talent! How exactly he caught your expression!"

"Really? You, I think, came out beautifully."

"When will the canvas be ready?"

"Gentlemen, it is late."

"Now for dinner. Let's go."

The Congress became animated. Talleyrand arose and stretched himself, Metternich smilingly picked up his portfolio from the floor, nonchalantly put on his fur cloak, which had been carelessly thrown across the back of a chair, and in leisurely fashion reached for his cane. Monsieur Isabey had grown weary of the delegates' rivalry over precedence. Despite their unnatural position during the sittings Monsieur Isabey depicted them on his canvas in unconstrained poses. The President's chair remained vacant: there was to be no center to the canvas. The actual work took place in Monsieur Isabey's studio, during separate sittings. Now he was busy with the general plan of the picture.

The delegates, leaving the hall in lively conversation or admiring the composition, paid compliments to the artist. Monsieur Isabey thanked them courteously, gave their remarks his extraordinary attention and invariably agreed with them. In instances of this nature his appearance conveyed the impression that their observations were most ingenious.

Those delegates who at parting addressed him as "dear Isabey" received a reply in the same patronizing tone, and were addressed by name. The artist paid no attention to the effect of his reply—the insulted, surprised face of the delegate.

Having drawn a cover over his canvas Monsieur Isabey went to the next room, where a washstand had been prepared for him. The lackey disdainfully poured water over the artist's hands.

Monsieur Isabey chatted with the lackey in broken German and told him something pleasant. He did this on principle, believing in the absolute necessity of using compliments in dealing with people.

Monsieur Isabey, not consciously, but somewhere at the bottom of his soul, thought all
people mentally deranged.

Having finished his conversation about yesterday's performance in the Burg theatre Razumovsky started to leave the Hall of Congress. In
the vestibule, near the stairs, he saw Monsieur
Isabey talking with one of the less important
delegates.

"Yes, Your Excellency, to my extreme sorrow
I must assign you a place not at the table, but
behind the table," he was saying with a tender
expression. "Just a little behind the table. However, to you—and probably to you alone—this is
of no import at all. Your soul is too lofty, Your
Excellency, to attach the slightest importance to
these unimportant matters of precedence."

"Certainly, to me, personally, it is of no import
at all," gloomily answered the delegate. "But I
am representing my state and I confess the place
you have assigned me in the picture somewhat
surprises me. My dear Monsieur Isabey, the picture has an official character, you know."

Isabey nodded meekly. "But you are standing
in line with the portrait of Emperor Franz! Do
you not value this fact, Your Excellency?" he said

with strength of voice, seemingly happy over his new argument. "It was my intention to emphasize the significance of your state, as well as the position which you hold in the Congress through your intellect and ability. Please take cognizance of the fact, Your Excellency, that you have been placed *en face,* not in profile. This also is important," Monsieur Isabey was saying, smiling towards Razumovsky as he approached them. "Do you know that if the Duke of Wellington were to arrive at the Congress, I should be obliged to paint him at the extreme end of the picture, and in profile? Yes, the Duke of Wellington himself. Because there is no other place."

"What, may I ask, is the subject of the dispute?" asked Razumovsky.

"No dispute at all," promptly retorted the diplomat. "I am voicing my admiration to Monsieur Isabey; the composition of his canvas is being executed very cleverly."

He smiled sourly and departed. Monsieur Isabey, crushed, glanced at Razumovsky.

"What? Dissatisfied with his place?" asked Andrey Kirillovitch.

"I am completely exhausted," said Isabey with a gesture of resignation.

"Everyone is offended, hurt, discontented . . .

With the exception of you, Count," he added politely. "What would happen if Wellington were actually to arrive!"

"Would you really place him at the end of the picture?" Razumovsky inquired, skeptically.

"Where else could I put him? Perhaps, the Lord permitting, this is but a rumor and he won't arrive. It would be impossible to rearrange everything at the last moment. Let him stand in profile, near the door, as though he had just arrived. But I do not know what to tell him. I will tell him that in profile he resembles Henry IV."

"I don't see any resemblance."

"Nor do I."

"Neither in countenance nor in intellect."

"This I do not dare express concerning a person of his rank. Neither do I dare contradict you. . . . Nor to accuse you of prevarication, Your Excellency. . . ." Monsieur Isabey added with deference.

They walked towards the exit, very pleased with each other. The attendant without a mace helped them with their fur coats. The attendant with a mace swung the doors wide. The last carriages were leaving by way of Ballplatz. Runners, in gala dress and feathered hats, preceded the carriages. They carried torches though it was not dark.

"Count. You have said nothing about my picture," Isabey remarked slyly as they reached the street.

"Shall we walk?"

"Don't you like the picture?"

"On the contrary. Very much," answered Razumovsky. "And I am pleased that you are painting it. You know how I admire and appreciate your great talent. But I do not particularly care for miniatures. In my opinion, miniatures develop a peculiar attitude towards life. They see everything on a small scale. Therefore, they see smallness in everything. The miniature has no future."

"In my opinion, the art of miniature is the highest. Because . . . I do not know how to explain it. Art should not be subservient. For instance, you worship Canova. . . . He is, without a doubt, a talented man. His art is very elegant. In your opinion, does Canova have a future? I think none. A huge naked Napoleon with a statue of Liberty in his hand inspires, in my opinion, nothing but laughter. I have sketched Napoleon about twenty times on snuffboxes. Very possibly this is nothing extraordinary. But honestly, Canova's Napoleon is not worth one of my snuffboxes."

"Aren't your miniatures too elegant?" Razumovsky objected with an imposing gesture. He suffered Canova's insult.

"Elegant, yes, to a degree. If punctuality is the courtesy of kings, precision in the minute details of a picture is, in my opinion, the courtesy of an artist. I am criticized for my attention to details in a picture? The problem of art is to portray and animate. One is impossible without the other. One must squeeze the water out of art. Aridity is a defect in everything but the art of painting. The future belongs to that art which will successfully assume the aspect of a bibelot.

"Elegance? One cannot do without it. Art is always more elegant than life, otherwise it would be unbearable. However, the Napoleon of my latest snuffboxes is hardly elegant: a tired, elderly man who endured everything from life."

"That is why, my dear Monsieur Isabey, you foresaw the fall of the Empire," Razumovsky said with a touch of irony. "When you drew the Corsican you undoubtedly had a presentiment that a year later you would be painting us. Of course I'm jesting," he added hastily.

"Take into consideration, my dear Count," said Monsieur Isabey, "that before painting the Corsican, who, incidentally, had more wisdom than all the inhabitants of the Burg, with the Ballplatz thrown in, I also painted various revolutionaries, and among them good men; and that before the revolutionaries, I painted the unfortunate Queen

Marie Antoinette. She was a beautiful woman.
Politicians live for one purpose, to cut one another's throats. That is not my fault. My purpose
is to paint as well as possible, and that's all. Pos-
terity will hardly be interested in my political
views. Isn't that so?"

"I hope I have not offended you," said Razumovsky. "We professional politicians have nothing
to boast of. By the way, have you heard of the
latest activity of your friend, Prince Talleyrand?
He proposes to the Congress that on the twenty-
first of January, the day of King Louis XVI's execu-
tion, a solemn Mass be read in the cathedral of
St. Stephen. . . . My word! I must say, we have
seen much; but when this man, a former inveterate
revolutionary, the friend and chum of all the Con-
ventions—king killers—made his motion, the hall
was enveloped in grave silence. We were as embarrassed as schoolgirls. Of course, the motion
was passed."

"Of course. I know. I was commissioned to work
out the ceremonial for the twenty-first of January.
However, all this does not prevent Talleyrand
from being the most charming man in the world,"
replied Monsieur Isabey. "He can betray his best
friend, but so beautifully that the betrayal inspires admiration. . . . Are you also on your way
to the palace, Count? I am in a hurry to attend

a rehearsal. Thus my life passes," sighed Monsieur Isabey. "From one pantomime to another."

"That's always so, Monsieur Isabey. What are you producing today?"

"We are producing 'Olympus.' I cast the gods very successfully, but no one dared play Venus. Some from modesty, some from fear of ridicule. . . . I found a way out. Venus will stand with her back to the audience. I easily succeeded in finding a lady who resembles Venus in the back. She is a lady-in-waiting, Mademoiselle Willem. At the conclusion of the pantomime there will be a musical fantasy, the music having been composed by Queen Hortense. Why must you be at the palace so early?"

"I must introduce to the Czar and Czarina a pathetic composer, Beethoven. His concert will take place soon. We must collect some money for the poor fellow. Unfortunately he is not in Emperor Franz' good graces. . . . The Prussian king will send ten ducats for his ticket. I know him. Others—I hope they will accept theirs. All my faith is in the Czar. The trouble is that it is so hard to converse with him," said Razumovsky, worried. "The Emperor Alexander, you know, is hard of hearing, and my protégé is stone deaf."

"Composer?" surprisedly asked Monsieur Isabey.

"Yes. It is unfortunate," sighed Razumovsky.

"How terrible!" replied Monsieur Isabey, closing his eyes in sympathy. "Now, Count, I am neither Emperor nor King but I will do everything I can. Tell this . . . what did you call him? . . . tell him to send me a ticket, in a brotherly spirit, as one artist to another. Is he a good composer?"

"Thank you," Razumovsky said kindly. He was moved. "Is he a good composer? To say excellent or marvelous would be stupid. I will answer you thus. He is my last chance for immortality. If, one hundred years from now, people remember me, it will be only because this man dedicated two of his symphonies to me."

Monsieur Isabey looked at Razumovsky. "So," he said, saddened. "Very interesting. *Sehr fidel, sehr fidel,*" [1] he added, and paused. Monsieur Isabey knew that the word *fidel* was used by the Germans not with the same meaning as in French and he used it at random, with seeming pleasure.

"Again *fidel*. You're abusing it, dear Monsieur Isabey," laughingly remarked Razumovsky. "Just as Lord Castlereagh abuses the word 'features.' Perhaps you have noticed that he cannot utter a phrase without this 'features.'"

[1] Very jolly, very jolly.

IV

I met Beethoven in Teplitz. His gift amazed me. Unfortunately he is an absolutely uncontrollable man. He is not entirely wrong in regarding the world as loathsome. But he will not succeed in making the world less unbearable, either for himself or for others.

—FROM A LETTER OF GOETHE

MONSIEUR OMER had directed the pantomime. Only a very humorless person could fail to use his name as a pun. Beaming with joy, Monsieur Isabey chatted with Omer and congratulated him upon the brilliant success of the tableaux; the pantomime had been performed superbly. The amateur actors adored the artist: he invariably enlivened them with his jollity. Even his critical remarks hurt no one's feelings. They were offered in such a kind spirit. He warmly thanked the participants in the pantomime and bestowed a kiss upon one young lady whom he especially favored (he favored nearly all of them), pleading his age as an excuse. This provoked general protest.

Strains of a march came from the ballroom. The intermission before the songs was of short duration. Scenery was being shifted hastily. Two lovers tiptoed in front of the stage and rehearsed their scene under Monsieur Isabey's supervision. He hummed the strain of their number. Both the melody and the sight of the enamored couple afforded him genuine pleasure.

A bell sounded. "Don't get excited. For God's sake, don't get excited," admonished the director in a fierce voice.

The lovers paled. Monsieur Isabey looked at Omer with reproach. Such ignorance of human nature amazed him. He smiled, tapped the young man's shoulder and paid the girl a compliment: Never before had he seen her look so charming. "How envious I am of that young blade What a lucky young princeling!" he said merrily and walked towards his post, behind the scenes. The curtain rose as the orchestra began playing the melody. The couple joined hands. Now Monsieur Isabey was confident that everything would run smoothly. His mission was at an end. "I must decide how to leave the ballroom without attracting attention," he thought, leaving his point of observance "Probably this way, then through the hall." Monsieur Isabey did not as yet know his way through the countless halls of the Burg. He

descended the steps, passed a corridor, turned
somewhere, followed another passage and found
himself in a red, gilded salon where, to his disappointment, people were playing cards—evidently those of the guests who were interested
neither in tableaux nor songs. At one of the tables,
with their backs towards Monsieur Isabey, a few
spectators were watching a game. At that table
played Prince Talleyrand, the best whist player
in Europe. Monsieur Isabey, smiling amiably,
circled the table. Before him flashed a deadly
pale, apathetic, lifeless face. He shuddered. At
the table a double of Maximilien Robespierre
was playing cards with German princes. The re-
pulsive features had always horrified Monsieur
Isabey. In the far-away days of the Revolution,
while yet a young man, Monsieur Isabey had
often seen Robespierre at a close distance.

The strains of music grew louder. Monsieur
Isabey finally reached the chain of halls where, at
the conclusion of the singing, the polonaise was to
be staged, with the Russian Czar and the Austrian Empress leading. The program of the ball
also had been prepared by Monsieur Isabey.

The singing was reaching a climax. . . . "I
am afraid I'll be late. Perhaps it would be better
not to go in. They may applaud me," thought
Monsieur Isabey modestly.

In the smaller hall a lady wearing a sky-blue
gown (the fashionable green had just been succeeded by a sky-blue, newly arrived from Paris)
was selling tickets for charity. The proceeds were
intended for the benefit of the slaves who were
so ill treated by the Mohammedans. Monsieur
Isabey knew the lady, the daughter of a British
admiral. He approached the table, obtained a
ticket and put as much money in the box as was
customary for one of his circumstances—perhaps
even a little more. Monsieur Isabey was very kind
and generous. He was sorry for the slaves, and the
English girl was beautiful. The box contained a
heap of gold and banknotes. Previously. behind
the scenes, Monsieur Isabey had heard that both
emperors had contributed one thousand ducats
each. Smiling, he chatted with the lady, who anxiously watched his every glance. Monsieur Isabey was very proud of his reputation as fashion
oracle and knew that his opinion of her toilette interested her tremendously. He purposely kept her
in suspense, remarking after a while that she was
dressed like a goddess. The English lady glowed
with happiness.

There was a burst of applause. As the lackey
flung the doors open a man in dark clothes rushed
out of the hall. His clothes were in sharp contrast
with those of the other guests. He stopped, embar-

rassed, cast a caustic glance over the table covered with gold coins, passed the Englishwoman, the lackey, and proceeded at a rapid pace. Count Razumovsky appeared at the doors simultaneously. "Where are you going? What is the matter?" he inquired in German, with a tone of reproach, as he overtook the man. Monsieur Isabey surmised that he was the German musician of whom Razumovsky had spoken.

The man was of small stature with a sad, pockmarked face. His old-fashioned coat bore the marks of long wear and his red cravat had been tied carelessly in keeping with his general slovenly appearance. "What an ugly man!" Monsieur Isabey thought with compassion. With his unerring glance he took in every detail about the old man including the thick, black hair, poorly cut "à la Titus" and the short fingers. "One should paint his portrait," Monsieur Isabey decided with suddenness.

"The music of Queen Hortense evidently far from delights him." The applause continued. "Great success! Everything is excellent!" Monsieur Isabey walked towards the hall. At the door he looked back and met the gaze of the German musician. The eyes of the composer. black, unusually bright, lay in sockets under sharply knit brows. His face was distorted with animosity and suffering. Razumovsky was telling him something, with a beseeching expression. "Indeed, what an amazing face," thought Monsieur Isabey.

V

THE FIRE was noticed late in the evening. Razumovsky was not at home. With the advent of Christmas the activities of the Congress approached their climax; no one retired before daylight. People rushed from one festivity to another. Confused messengers, sent by their confused Superintendent, located Andrey Kirillovitch with difficulty. When his carriage, drawn by the horses at great speed, reached the palace, the main building, that portion of the palace which contained the picture gallery, Canova's hall and the world-famous library, was in flames. The red reflection in the sky could be seen from all parts of Vienna.

Confusion prevailed in the square in front of the palace. From a side street a detachment of infantry approached the scene at a rapid pace. Mounted policemen carried torches, blowing their bugles. Two horses galloped through the open gate of the garden carrying an enormous waterbarrel. The sound of breaking glass arose above the general noise. For a moment the palace disappeared in clouds of black smoke. A tremendous flame burst forth, illuminating the square with a grim, dark-red light.

Razumovsky's coachman, shouting and whimpering in the same breath, had difficulty in controlling the horses. Andrey Kirillovitch arose, intending to say something, changed his mind, sat down and got up again. The Superintendent, upon seeing Razumovsky, waved his hands and ran toward the Count's coach. A piece of burning wood flew high over the roof and fell near the carriage, sizzling in the trampled snow. The horses shied. Razumovsky, upon descending from the carriage, nearly fell. The Superintendent supported the Count and irresponsibly shouted at the driver. The sound of bugles, the neighing of horses, and the rumbling and crackling of the blazing palace made it impossible to talk. Andrey Kirillovitch gazed despairingly at the Superintendent, then over the latter's fur hat at the destruction of his home. "Your Excellency! What a misfortune!" the Superintendent was saying with tears in his voice. "Your Excellency! My God! When Johann came to me with the horrible news I rushed out, like one insane. . . . My wife, also. I ordered them to send for you, Your Excellency. . . . Then the sight of . . . Oh, my God!"

The fire chief in charge of the rescue work hurried to the Count, saluted and, in answer to the Count's silent question, waved his hands like a physician at the bedside of a dying patient.

"It may be possible to save the other building," he said, pointing vaguely. His appearance seemed to say, "Of course, I can't tell you the real truth—but you can guess—by degrees. . . "

"But this one here—is more important! This one here!" said Razumovsky, with despair. "If it is impossible to save the building, save the . . ." His voice broke "We shall do everything possible," the fire chief answered in a sympathetic tone. "The real work was done in the garden. We made a German knot and are tossing everything through the windows. . . . The pictures . . ."

It took Andrey Kirillovitch some time to realize what a German knot was and how his pictures had been tossed from the windows. A mounted fireman galloped over to the fire chief and, bending down, made some report. The fire chief's face expressed concern. He walked hastily towards the gate. Andrey Kirillovitch looked at the Superintendent anxiously as though wondering what he should do and what he should ask him.

"Where did it start? What's the cause?"

"The heating system, Your Excellency, the damned pipe-heating!" answered the Superintendent in despair. "I warned you, Your Excellency!"

Andrey Kirillovitch did not remember any warning issued by his Superintendent about the pipe-heating. But he understood. The fire had been caused by the pipes, which were laid under the floors. The very installation he had flaunted before the Viennese as the latest word in equipment.

"Well . . . what should we do, then? What should we do?" asked Razumovsky. He saw another barrel going through the gates and decided that he should go to the garden. The Superintendent accompanied him. Hissing embers were falling incessantly.

In the garden, behind the gate, the pathways were covered with fragments of glass. The firemen had broken the windows, as well as the glass walls of the nursery. "That's nothing . . . we can restore the nursery," bravely thought Andrey Kirillovitch. "We can restore the nursery." There was less noise in the garden than on the square.

Despite a moonless night the scene was as bright as daylight due to the reflection of the fire and the firemen's torches. The thick clouds of smoke were following another direction. At the main entrance of the hall, on the fire bed, were the water pumps. Around them, people in queer costumes, bloused, and helmeted, were working feverishly. Three fine, narrow streams of water were directed almost straight up in the air, flooding the upper story and main stairway. The carved door, smashed to pieces, lay half-embedded in the snow. Andrey Kirillovitch watched the streams of water with eager hope. He wanted to tell the firemen to send at least one stream to the mezzanine, but changed his mind, not having the courage to issue orders. "They know better. They are fine, experienced men. . . ."

At his left, where the fire was less violent, Razumovsky saw what the fire chief called a German knot. Firemen inside the palace were throwing articles through a canvas chute which was extended from a palace window and fastened to the thill of a cart. Shadows of men in helmets could be seen from time to time at the window.

"What men! What courageous fellows!" Andrey Kirillovitch thought with genuine gratitude. The canvas chute bent in the center, then straightened out. Something heavy slid, fell and cracked. Razumovsky gasped and ran toward the cart. In the dirty, melting snow, in broken frames, lay his pictures, charred and torn. "My God! And the Titians!" Razumovsky muttered. He clutched his head, walked to a bench and sat down weakly. "What mockery!" he thought. "My whole life reduced to dust. . . ."

A pair of horses pulled a truck of a peculiar shape through the open gate. The firemen jumped off, adjusted several parts and the truck was transformed into an enormous ladder with beautifully forged hooks. The ladder was quickly set against the wall, its hooks grappling the balcony rail. One of the firemen jumped, balanced himself on a rung, testing the strength of the balcony rails. The ladder was solid. One after another, men in helmets climbed the rungs rapidly, adroitly.

"What skill! How wonderful they are! I must reward them," Andrey Kirillovitch said to himself, realizing in the next moment that complete ruin lay ahead for him. His palace and objects of art, collected during a lifetime, were priceless. For the moment he forgot about his intention of presenting the palace to the Emperor. "What shall I do? What shall I do? It's not my fault," he was saying over and over again. "I'll live somewhere, far away. People will not forsake me. My Emperor will help me. Perhaps move to a hotel? No. In Zum Roemischen Kaiser one can't even find a dog-hole now!" He knew that to leave the scene of the fire was out of the question, even though he was of no assistance. He wanted to go to bed. He was extremely tired, cold and shivering. "It will be a miracle if I don't catch cold. . . . What is this?" At a large water tank, at the side wing of the main building, there were two lines of men. Some handed one another full buckets of water, while others returned the empty ones. "Where do they come from? Who are they?" Then Andrey Kirillovitch remembered that all Viennese guilds of carpenters and masons were obliged, by law to assist at a fire. "Indeed, they are well organized. Good, delightful people." Suddenly he turned, horror-stricken. From behind, there came the frantic neighing of horses. Stablemen were dragging with great difficulty blindfolded horses from the stables, which were already aglow. "What a fine idea to blindfold horses! How did they think of it? Oh, Lord, what a wind! This means that Canova Hall is doomed! And Flora!" . . .

Carriages continued to approach the palace. The news of a fire in Vienna's finest palace had reached the receptions and balls with surprising speed.

Cordons of troops encircled the square, halting the carriages. Gaily attired people, their faces happy and excited, left their carriages, stared at the fire-enveloped palace with eager curiosity and exchanged remarks.

"What a misfortune for the Count." "This is terrible." "Neither the Burg nor Schoenbrunn has such treasures of art." "Is it really impossible to save anything?" "After all, our fire force is not very efficient." "They have the same in Paris Do you remember the fire at the Schwartzenbergs'?" "All this happened because of that French heating system." "We were attending the ball at Esterhazy's, and suddenly heard of it." "We were just about to dine." "A dreadful sight, but it is beautiful, don't you think?" "On the contrary. Nothing is beautiful about it. I swallowed so much smoke." "Poor Count, I ought to shake hands with him." "Oh yes, but where is he?"

Upon learning the whereabouts of the Count a number of the people directed their steps towards the garden at the side gate. Razumovsky still sat on the bench and watched with a dull and seemingly indifferent expression. The fire at that time had gained impetus, due to the strong wind and despite the desperate efforts of the firemen.

The newly arrived hesitated uncomfortably, not knowing how to behave themselves on such an occasion. Their social training had included everything except a fire. Some bowed to the Count with respectful sorrow and quickly retired. Others came near him and shook his hand in silence with more feeling than usual. Others endeavored to cheer him and talked of the heating system, the beauty of the palace, of how it could be reconstructed.

Despite the absurdity of their condolences the general sympathy strengthened Andrey Kirillovitch somewhat. He regained his senses Coughing from the acrid smoke, he answered all expressions of sympathy. He even made an effort to appear calm.

Among those who arrived at the fire was Monsieur Isabey. The sight of the blazing palace had shocked him. Better than anyone did he know what treasures had been lodged in the palace. He approached Razumovsky and pressed his hand.

"Cher ami!" he said, but his overtaxed emotions did not allow him to finish the phrase. Tears appeared in his eyes. Andrey Kirillovitch arose and embraced the artist. He knew that Isabey not only offered sincere sympathy but himself shared the misfortune. He was not so much concerned about Razumovsky's feelings as he was grieved at the loss of these great works of art.

A flügel-adjutant on a black horse galloped into the garden. Instantly it was understood that the Emperor had arrived. "Which emperor?" "Emperor Alexander?" people were asking one another. "I told you His Majesty would arrive." "I did not think so. What an honor for the Count." "He has always been in great favor."

Andrey Kirillovitch, accompanied by the flügel-adjutant, walked quickly towards the gate. He could not fail to appreciate the honor done him. The firemen stopped their work for a moment and came to attention. Emperor Franz was enter-

ing the gateway, followed by a small number of
attendants. He was in civilian dress, without a fur
coat, in a warm, cotton-wadded coat, silk hat and
Hessian boots. Everyone bowed respectfully. The
Emperor accelerated his pace when he saw Razumovsky approaching, and when they met offered
him both hands. It seemed to Andrey Kirillovitch
that the Emperor had intended embracing him but
had changed his mind. The palace fire, after all,
was not a sufficiently great catastrophe. Deeply
moved, Razumovsky thanked the Emperor. Despite the excitement, he expressed his gratitude in
conventional form, in French. The Emperor
answered in German. "My dear Count. This might
just as well have happened to my assembly hall.
We also have the 'Rohren' heating system."

"God forbid, Your Majesty," answered Razumovsky, changing to German.

"This comes from our aping the French. . . ."

Andrey Kirillovitch sighed. The Emperor
turned towards the palace. The firemen, after the
momentary intermission, worked now with re-
doubled energy. The fire chief mounted the ladder which leaned against the balcony. All hope of
saving the main building had been abandoned
and its collapse was expected momentarily. The
chief ordered his men to retreat to the side wing.

Monsieur Isabey, wiping his eyes, returned to

the square. The adjoining streets were flooded with spectators. Police officers held back the crowd, making exceptions, by gestures, for those who, by their appearance, belonged to the upper classes. Behind the lines, in the front row, Monsieur Isabey recognized the German musician whom Razumovsky had pointed out to him at the Empress's performance. The musician's face distressed him even more than at their first meeting. "A peculiar, wonderful head!" thought Monsieur Isabey. He left the police line and, meeting an acquaintance, talked of the fire. During the conversation, he turned more than once to look for the German musician. It occurred to him that he ought to memorize the details of this unusual face. "In case it be necessary to portray on canvas a gloomy, solemn inspiration, or something of that kind," thought Monsieur Isabey.

Part of the main wall collapsed with a sickening thud. A black cloud pierced by tongues of red flame, billowed to one side beyond the crumpled wall, against which the vast picture gallery was silhouetted, enveloped by smoke. Then a hideous rumbling was heard, and with a prolonged roar the majestic structure caved in. The palace was no more.

VI

Perfectio igitur et imperfectio revera modi solummodo cogitandi sunt, nempe notiones, quas fingere solemus ex eo quod eijusdem speciei aut generis individua ad invicem comparamus.

—SPINOZA

ON THIS particular morning the snakes were being fed in the traveling zoo. The owner, a Koenigsburg German, who had roamed the world for many years and now called himself a "trapper" (this word, then little known, added considerably to his importance), arose early, had his breakfast, and, dressed in an odd hunting outfit, entered the room which housed the boa constrictor. The room was warm and humid. The boa liked the heat.

The trapper approached the box. It was made of very thick glass with a trapdoor on top surrounded by an iron grating on which there had been hung an inscription: "Please do not aggravate the boa constrictor." But the inscription and the grating were there for the sole purpose of playing on the audience's nerves. The trapper knew that the serpent was tame, would not break the glass nor attack the people. As the animal saw its owner, it crawled out from under the old blanket in anticipation of its feeding. Above its violet-gray coils with square, black spots protruded a thin, crooked neck. Divided by a black line, the head, with small, slanted eye-slits, was held steady in the direction of the trapdoor.

"You'll wait," said the trapper, admiring the snake.

A bell was sounded at the gate. A tradeswoman brought a few rabbits. She did not enter the small garden but, cautiously eyeing the shack, wished the trapper a pleasant good morning. She told him about the previous night's fire, not far from there. The palace of the rich Russian Erzherzog had been completely razed.

"The embers are still glowing . . . and how many people are there," said the tradeswoman. "Even the Emperor was there. No one is allowed on the square. All those people are coming from the fire."

The trapper yawned. He had seen many fires. He picked out the fattest rabbit, haggled about the price, and paid her.

"Will you really throw the poor thing to the snake alive?" the woman asked, looking with pity at the rabbit. "There are so many kinds of animals, aren't there?"

"It is a matter of taste," mumbled the trapper. "We eat dead meat. They eat theirs alive. But this one eats once in two weeks."

"Good Lord!"

"He can go without food for two months, only he loses weight and is disgruntled," explained the trapper, who loved his animal. Holding the rabbit in his left hand he walked through the gate, and viewed the passing people, debating whether or not it would be worth while calling them in. The majority of the passers-by were common people, though there were some of the better class. Several stopped, curiously examined the poster and the peculiar man, making fun of his Prussian accent. Some hesitated and walked on. Others tried to look through the gate. Two men paid admission—the first one a soldier, the other of higher class.

"A government official or a teacher," thought the trapper, who liked to analyze his customers according to their appearance.

"Most interesting! A frightful spectacle! An enormous Mexican boa constrictor as long as four men put together. He kills people with one stroke of his tail! Chokes tigers and buffaloes with no effort whatsoever!" lied the trapper. "There are snakes, crocodiles and jaguars! The feeding of the boa constrictor will take place immediately! He swallows live rabbits! A frightful spectacle! He screams with joy and sings."

A short pock-marked man standing by the poster with a hand cupped to his ear listened to the trapper.

"Sings?" he inquired abruptly.

"He whistles and screams. It sounds like singing," replied the trapper. He examined the pock-marked gentleman from head to foot but could not determine his occupation. However, he decided that he was "small fry." "It sounds like singing," he repeated, louder, as he noticed that the gentleman was hard of hearing. "In ancient Mexico they listened to the voice of the boa constrictor. They were considered sacred animals. Come in, please. You'll be satisfied. . . ."

The pock-marked gentleman muttered something, rummaged in his pocketbook, extracted a coin, and entered the small garden where the soldier and clerk were exchanging glances. The trapper glanced disdainfully at the remainder of the people, nodded to the tradeswoman and closed the gate.

"It sings? The boa constrictor?" the short man asked again.

"Snakes are very musical," said the trapper,

stroking the rabbit. "Presently you'll see the Indian snakes. They are, perhaps, more musical than
you and I. They are charmed by flute playing.
They coil, dance, go into a stupor. Then one can
do anything with them." The gentleman's face
became distorted. "Only the Indian ones do not
sing. Of the whole snake species only the boa con-
strictors sing. Usually, when they are fed. Feeding
is the main thing to them. . . . He is always dissatisfied . . if something doesn't suit him. That's
probably why he sings . . . sings," he repeated,
and, opening the door, invited the visitors inside
the shack.

"No, thank you—after you," said the clerk,
laughingly. The trapper also laughed. Concealing
the rabbit under his coat, he entered first. The
others followed. Everyone came near the box. The
serpent's head was swinging over a cone formed
by the coils of his body.

"Sacrament!" the clerk was saying, shrinking
back. "Jesus Maria! Jesus Maria!" repeated the soldier. The short man was looking at the monster
with horror.

The trapper pulled over a step ladder with one
hand and took the shivering rabbit from under his
coat. "Listen," said the gentleman, holding the
trapper by the hand (only now did he understand
what was happening), "don't throw . . . I'll pay

you . . ." The trapper looked at the pock-marked gentleman perplexedly. However, he was accustomed to people, especially ladies, showing compassion for the rabbit at the last moment before it was fed to the snake.

"You and I must eat, sir," he replied. "So does the serpent. You, perhaps, eat oysters. They are alive." (This was his usual argument, which invariably impressed sympathetic visitors.) "How can I not feed him? It would be unfair to the customers. They paid money . . ."

A peculiar sound came from the box—neither a scream, nor a whistle. The snake perceived the rabbit. It changed position. Its eyes sparkled. Its neck bent into a shape not unlike that of a swan's. The little head quivered. The spectators gasped. "Indeed, that song is rather musical." The government clerk smiled at the short gentleman, with a sneer. He evidently knew him. "In its own way, the serpent is also a musician."

The gentleman looked angrily at the clerk, curtly said something and fastened his eyes on the cage. The trapper mounted the ladder, lifted the grating, opened the trap-door (there was a smell of musk), tossed the rabbit into the box and closed the trap-door instantly. The short gentleman screamed. The rabbit fell gently to the sand and, becoming electrified, met the serpent's eye. The snake repeated the peculiar sound. Its little eyes sparkled more brightly. The serpent threw the upper part of its body back, opened its jaws slowly and suddenly darted forward with its whole body, instantly unrolling its huge coils. The gentleman screamed again, covering his twitching face with his hands, and ran out of the little house.

VII

I had become very tired of seeing nothing but pictures.

—GOETHE

ANDREY KIRILLOVITCH RAZUMOVSKY
had lived in Italy for two years with his
wife and sister-in-law.

At the family council which met at Vienna in
the spring of 1822, Razumovsky made a report of
his financial condition. He read with confusion
something containing figures which sounded like
a brief report. He faltered, searching among the
columns of figures of income, debts, and interest
on debts. These figures had been prepared for the
Prince by his Superintendent. Andrey Kirillovitch
was informed very slightly concerning his affairs.
Some time ago he could hardly have enumerated
by heart the holdings which had been left him by
his father the Hetman. Now almost everything
had been sold, the money spent, and of what had
once been an enormous estate were left only remnants—or what seemed like remnants to Andrey
Kirillovitch.

Razumovsky read his report in French, which was very inconvenient. The words were either untranslatable—such as *volest* (a district including several villages), *ouyezd* (a smaller district), *desiantina* (a Russian acre), or they sounded foolish in French, like *revisional soul* (a serf). Andrey Kirillovitch had found it much easier to read reports about the organization of Europe before emperors and ministers. He knew the affairs of the governments of Europe better and in greater detail than his own. In addition, he felt very depressed. His wife, his sister-in-law and all his Austrian relatives had until then believed him to be "wealthy among the wealthy."

His family displayed very delicate interest. The failure was spoken of in a casual tone of voice, with a shade of gay surprise which was supposed to signify, "Hm-m-m. What an amusing story. We are poor!" but behind that casual tone Andrey Kirillovitch sensed disappointment. No one even thought of blaming Razumovsky; however, his conscience hurt him—having married a young Austrian countess of thirty-three, himself sixty, he had no business to be poor.

After the report, his Vienna relatives offered Andrey Kirillovitch a few practical suggestions. One devised a profitable financial venture, transforming rubles into ducats, but when this was

checked, he had confused silver rubles with bank
notes. Another advised a mortgage on Baturin—
that property had a first and second mortgage and
the figures had been mentioned three or four times
in Andrey Kirillovitch's report. The third deci-
sively proposed throwing the creditors out neck
and crop. This the Prince was doing of his own
accord. True, only figuratively. As time passed, the
discussion, accounts and failure of the proposed
ventures tired the relatives and all agreed to what
Andrey Kirillovitch, with a heartache, proposed.
He intended closing his Vienna palace, which had
been rebuilt after the fire, without its former
grandeur, discharging his staff of servants, except,
perhaps about ten most needed and devoted ones,
and settling in Italy.

One of the young Thurheins, who had recently
returned from Rome, heartily approved of this
plan and, as proof, quoted a few of the restaurant
prices in Rome. Prince Razumovsky listened with
a sad smile. For the first time in his life he was
obliged to hear such things. Of course, the price
of oysters and wines was of no import, but the fact
was that in Italy one could do without one hundred servants, without fifty horses in the stables,
large receptions, and everything that the style of
living, the social circle and connections of the
Razumovskys demanded as absolutely necessary.

After his proposal was accepted Andrey Kirillo-vitch felt better. He kissed the hands of his wife and sister-in-law very tenderly and was grateful for their not being angry. Indeed, Razumovsky felt guilty; yet the expressions on their faces some-what irked him, particularly their exaggerated, delicate courtesy. The thought flashed through his mind that, after all, he was hardly responsible to-wards his sister-in-law as well as towards the other Thurheins who, together with himself, had squan-dered the enormous fortune of Hetman Kirill Grigorievitch. But this thought lingered for only a second. He loved his wife and her relatives.

His family busied themselves with preparations for departure. It was decided that they should stay a while in Verona because the International Con-gress was now in session there; in Rome because it's Rome; and in Naples because King Ferdinand, a boon-companion of Razumovsky, lived there. Andrey Kirillovitch had been Ambassador at his court more than forty years before.

Upon leaving Vienna, Andrey Kirillovitch, his wife and sister-in-law, planned, by unanimous consent, to live quietly, isolated in their intimate family circle, to neither invite guests nor accept invitations from others. However, during the first few laps of their journey it became very obvious that the intimate family circle was quite dull.

They loved each other but exhausted all themes
of conversation. In Italy the ladies became more
cheerful. The Congress of Verona was roaring
with activity, at a distance resembling in its splendor that of Vienna. The Razumovskys plunged
immediately into the circle of their international
acquaintances and did not emerge from it during
their sojourn in Italy. The Prince's frame of mind
grew sadder and sadder. He had seen so many
sights during his lifetime. At one of the Verona
receptions Chateaubriand, upon learning that the
Razumovskys expected to visit Rome, said to
Andrey Kirillovitch, in French, "Rome is a good
place to forget everything, despise everything and
die." Razumovsky well knew that Chateaubriand
had especial reason to be gloomy. He didn't have
a sou in his pocket. He was suffering from gout.
His latest works had not met with success. His
intimate affairs were most entangled. He did not
know whom he loved—Madame Recamier, Madame de Durass or Madame Arbuthnot (others
even went so far as to gossip that he loved his wife,
but they were laughed at). Nevertheless this
saying of the famous man impressed Andrey Kirillovitch very deeply.

In Rome Razumovsky attended the *Tenebræ*
services in the Sistine Chapel and, while listening
to the music, dwelt on the fact that his career was

at an end as well as his life and that he had nothing to wait for. The title of Prince, which he had received during the session of the Congress of Vienna, was his last success and the fire at his palace had deprived him of his former interest in life.

After the services his wife and sister-in-law talked long and constantly on the superiority of the Catholic religion. Andrey Kirillovitch pretended not to hear. He knew how passionately the Thurheins desired to convert him to Catholicism.

That evening they visited the Lievens, with whom they had become very friendly in Rome. Countess Lieven, after repeated requests, read one of her letters written on blue paper. They were being much discussed in Europe. In the letter the Countess spoke of the Revolution and she incidentally used a maxim, borrowed, by the way, from Wellington.

The maxim impressed Razumovsky as foolish (he felt that the whole letter had been written for the express purpose of glorifying the maxim). "In that case the Royal equestrians could liberate the world from distress," he thought pessimistically. "Why does she always bother with politics? Such nonsense. And the blue paper is nonsense. Her eyes probably don't hurt her but she writes on blue paper so that, in conversation, people will

remark, 'Countess Lieven writes on blue paper.'"
He had intended to take issue with her; to frighten
the Countess with the possibility of a new revolution—but he didn't. He was too tired. Furthermore
he admired Countess Lieven for her intellect,
breeding, and elegant manners, which he especially
valued. King Ferdinand, who had met him with
his usual jovial laughter, on the contrary, impressed Razumovsky as an example of vulgarity.
Andrey Kirillovitch looked at his old acquaintance
with curiosity and thought it strange that he, a
grandson of a Little-Russian herdsman, objected
to the manners of a descendant of Louis XIV.

At an auction in Rome a Raphael was being sold
for three thousand ducats. Razumovsky had no
spare money and the Raphael was carried off by
an Englishman who obviously knew nothing of
painting. Poverty was oppressing Andrey Kirillovitch. His health was poor. His heart behaved just
as badly. The doctors prescribed a strict diet. The
carrying out of the diet was attended to by his
wife and sister-in-law, who were increasingly
alarmed about his condition. All this irritated him.
His mental state affected his family. It grew dull.
To escape boredom they decided to adopt a little
girl.

The only consolation left for Andrey Kirillovitch
was music. He attended the opera frequently, ad-

mired the Italian voices, reluctantly praising
Rossini, who by that time had eclipsed all other
composers and was acclaimed the sovereign of
them all. In his declining years Andrey Kirillovitch resumed his violin playing. He played in the
evening when he was alone. The ladies went to
the theater or visited their friends every evening
while, according to his doctor's orders, he was
obliged to stay indoors as much as possible and
retire early. Razumovsky gave Rossini his due but
preferred the music of Beethoven, who by that
time had long been out of vogue. Andrey Kirillovitch did not play too well. He attempted themes
from symphonies and quartettes. His favorites
were Russian quartettes which had been dedicated to him by his old friend, and among them
the Adagio of the Seventh Quartette. He, himself,
had acquainted Beethoven with the Russian melody of that particular composition. At times he
thought he was not gifted at all and that fact was
the principal misfortune of his life. He loved art,
had a finer appreciation of it than most people but
was unable to create anything himself. "Too much
taste and not enough creative ability is unfortunate, indeed."

While in Naples Razumovsky unexpectedly received a letter from St. Petersburg with news of
the death of his brother, Peter. The message

shocked him despite the fact that with advancing years he was becoming hardened and had grown accustomed to the departure of those near him. Since their boyhood days they had seldom met. Peter Kirillovitch had lived in St. Petersburg—but they loved each other. His wife and sister-in-law shared Razumovsky's grief. They ceased going to the theater and refused invitations. But in their eyes he could detect a carefully veiled joy. Peter Kirillovitch had had no legitimate children and Razumovsky was entitled to the greater part of his fortune. Andrey Kirillovitch could not conscientiously blame his wife and sister-in-law. They had not even known Peter Kirillovitch. However, their conversations about his deceased brother awakened in him a feeling of sadness. From their casual questions it was evident that they knew which properties remained and their approximate value. There was nothing unnatural in this. He himself, with all his love for his brother, could not help but feel relieved now that the opportunity to reëstablish their former style of living for his wife and sister-in-law had presented itself. Nevertheless when Lulu Thurhein, concealing her happiness under a mask of complete indifference, ridiculously distorted Russian names—Gostilitzy, Arkadak, names of the properties in Pakov, Toula and Moscow—Razumovsky had to restrain his anger and make an effort not to say anything insulting.

The particulars of the inheritance arrived in the spring of 1824. Peter Kirillovitch had died rather unexpectedly and had not thought of making his will until the last minute. The text of the will was taken down at the Count's request, by Speransky himself. Speransky was, at that time, the highest authority on Russian law, but in the rush did not use accurate wording. The will undoubtedly would have been declared illegal had not the government clerk, Krinkowsky, come across a grave mistake made by the famous government barrister. The inheritance was enormous. Unlike his brother, Peter Kirillovitch had never spent so much as the interest on his great fortune.

Before long the Prince's wife and sister-in-law began to suggest moving from Italy to Paris. Only in Paris were there conveniences, genuine society and good physicians. Razumovsky did not protest. It made but little difference to him where he was to spend his remaining days.

In order to attend to his inheritance and other affairs the Prince was obliged to go to Vienna. Not without argument and objections did the ladies agree to let him go alone. From there he was to go to Paris. It was decided, nevertheless, to await warm weather. From the southern, Italian climate to that of central Europe was too sudden a change and seemed dangerous for one of Razumovsky's age. While waiting for his departure, Andrey Kirillovitch again began buying various objects of art. The Raphael eluded him, but there were other bargains. At first he bought with enthusiasm, picturing in his mind how everything would look and be placed in his new home. Then he grew tired and even ashamed of it. "At the age of seventy-two with one foot in the grave, one needs but Tomir's bronze to be completely happy." In the latter part of April, Andrey Kirillovitch left Naples. At his wife's insistence he traveled slowly, stopping often on his way, and arrived in Vienna on the 7th of May, 1824.

Razumovsky's palace, having been closed for two years, needed cleaning and alterations. Andrey Kirillovitch had about twenty relatives and close friends with whom he could stop during his sojourn in Vienna.

Almost unconsciously, perhaps because he was provoked with the members of his own family, he stopped, not with the Thurheins, but with the Thunes, relatives of his first wife. He had continued his bonds of friendly relationship with them even after his second marriage. Razumovsky's arrival had been anticipated. He was received with open arms by the Thunes, Thurheins, Lichovskys, Hesses, Pergains, Klam-Martinetzes.

Upon finding himself in the old familiar environment which he associated with the best years of his life, Andrey Kirillovitch livened up somewhat. While he was taking his bath and making his toilette his relatives were whispering with concern about how the Prince had aged. After brief discussion and research, by marriages and funerals, it became evident that Razumovsky was at least seventy—perhaps even older. The ladies sighed, surprised. Not so long ago Erzherzog Andreas was the recognized Conqueror of Hearts. His conquests were recalled with smiles. "Is it possible! Seventy!"

The heavy atmosphere cleared away when Razumovsky, immaculately dressed, with carefully powdered hair (hardly anyone powdered any more) made his appearance.

He was in high spirits, insisted upon speaking Viennese, not French, and jested, as he distributed presents. He sensed, however, that his presents were not a great success, despite their polite admiration of the various pictures, medals and bronzes. "Perhaps I should stop at a fashion store and buy some neckties and fans," he thought.

The Thunes had arranged a large dinner party for the evening of his arrival. "Just for the family circle," explained his hostess. However, there were no less than thirty. When assembled, they listened

with admiration to Razumovsky's stories and anecdotes. He was a splendid storyteller and knew
anecdotes about all the famous people of the
world.

"I hope you don't regret missing the concert?"
the hostess asked one of her guests.

"Oh, no."

"What concert?" inquired Razumovsky. He
was told that Beethoven's grand concert was taking place that evening.

"We also were obliged to reserve a box on
Schindler's imposition, but, of course, we shan't be
there."

"What time does the concert begin?"

Razumovsky consulted his watch hurriedly.
What he was about to do was both improper and
tactless but he preferred to commit ten improper
acts rather than miss Beethoven's concert.

He launched into profuse apologies, which
neither his hostess nor the guests at first understood.

"My friend, what I am doing is *une gouja-
teria!* " [1] he said in French, kissing the hostess'
hand. "What can I do to obtain your pardon?" The
hostess forced a smile, assuring him that she understood. But from the expression on her face
Razumovsky could plainly see how his strange be-

[1] An ungentlemanly act.

havior had affected her. The guests looked at one another in embarrassment. They had been invited with Razumovsky as the evening's attraction.

"But how, my dear Prince, can you listen to music on an empty stomach?"

"Perhaps you will have a bite before the concert?"

His host had found the invitation. It read, in German: "The Grand Musical Concert of Herr Ludwig van Beethoven, on the seventh of May in *K.K. Hoftheatre naechst dem Kaertnerthore.*" This was followed by the program. "You know what? I have a compromise to offer," said his host. "It is the new Beethoven symphony that interests you so. It takes place at the end of the concert. Therefore you can have at least part of your dinner with us, and you will still be on time for the symphony. We shall dine immediately. Haven't I made a practical suggestion?"

"You certainly cannot refuse."

Indeed he could not refuse the compromise. The steward hurried to the kitchen and gave orders to the cooks. A carriage was ordered for the Prince. In the meantime the guests had entered the dining room.

"Your musical gluttony surprises me," remarked his hostess at the table. The Prince's decision to stay for a portion of the dinner eased the tension somewhat. "Have you not spent two years in Italy and heard their divine music?" Then Rossini became the subject of conversation. Not so long ago he had performed in Vienna and charmed everyone; a composer of genius, a conductor, pianist, singer! "He has a marvelous voice and, in addition, is such an amiable, gracious man. . . ." "At Metternich's reception he wrote impromptu more than sixty variations on one theme, into the guests' albums." "In London they covered him with gold."

"Also here."

"Do you know that he composed 'Othello' in twenty days?"

"It is very evident," said Razumovsky, smiling. The ladies became vociferous in their reproaches. "I take it all back. I admire him very much. Do you know that in Rome 'Othello' ends with the reconciliation of the Moor with Desdemona? They sing a love duet. But Rossini is not to blame for that. The public demands it. But the Italians sing beautifully, indeed."

"This evening, at the symphony, you will hear a remarkable singer—Henrietta Sontag," said his hostess. "I pray you—don't fall in love. . . . She is twenty, of great talent, and beautiful," she said with a slight smile.

"What? A singer at the symphony?"

"Haven't you heard? The Ninth Symphony is

announced with a chorus and vocal soloists. This, obviously, is Beethoven's innovation."

The conversation shifted to the composer. Andrey Kirillovitch questioned the Viennese with anxious curiosity about his old friend, whom he had lost sight of for a long time. The news was not pleasant. It was generally observed that he had failed in health, was completely deaf, had become an impossible person and drank. Others went so far as to call him a drunkard. His affairs were also in a bad state. The Prince's gay mood suddenly left him. The fact that they had called Beethoven, who was much younger than the Prince, an old man, cut him to the quick.

"You know, Beethoven almost left us," said the host. "Not so long ago he suddenly declared his intention of leaving Vienna. Then friends became very sentimental and begged him, by letter, to remain."

"In fact it would be a shame and a great loss for Vienna to lose such a man!"

"Let us face the truth. He dwells in the past and is about to lose his mind."

"Nevertheless, we ought to help the old man."

"I don't think so," a plump, round-faced lady said decidedly.

"I was passing the Café Mariahilf and saw him sitting on the terrace, drinking! If he has enough money for wine he should not arrange benefits and beg for donations."

"Severe but just."

"There are many paupers among the musicians. It would be nice but we can't help them all. It's impossible. One should contribute money only in case of dire need."

"Yes. But what do you call dire need, Mitzi? Beethoven is undoubtedly in need."

"In need of wine."

"Perhaps wine is necessary for inspiration," one of the young guests suggested humorously.

"I am surprised at you. That is what all drunkards claim. I am confident that Rossini composes without wine."

"I don't know about Rossini. As for myself, I compose marvelous verse when I take a few drinks. You don't believe me? Have it your own way." The guests laughed. Razumovsky was becoming more and more depressed. He knew that society held Beethoven in high esteem but could not really respect a musician who needed benefit concerts. Andrey Kirillovitch knew himself to be guilty of the same psychology—that of a rich man —but to find it in others annoyed him. The host mildly defended Beethoven from the attacks of the round-faced lady. He reminded her that Rossini himself held the old man in high esteem and cried like a baby when he heard his music. "When he visited Vienna one of his first duties was to call on Beethoven."

"And they say Beethoven welcomed him. God knows how! He advised Rossini to compose a few more 'Barbers of Seville'."

"That was not a bad suggestion."

"Yes. But what a rude man."

"Who told you that he was rude to Rossini? It's untrue."

"Someone told me. He didn't even return his call."

"If he didn't return the visit it is because he is a recluse."

"Very good. But what will foreigners think of us! I, myself, have heard Rossini implore Prince Metternich to do something for Beethoven."

"Think of whom you are speaking, Mitzi," the hostess' mother admonished sternly "Remember that Beethoven is deaf. To even dream of such a thing is dreadful."

The round-faced lady made no reply. Razumovsky looked at her with displeasure.

"It is as if you should be struck dumb," the hostess remarked jovially. "Just imagine: they would be discussing Vienna's gossip and you would be unable to add anything."

The lady laughed. Others joined her.

"That would be worse than Beethoven's deafness."

"It might be something from Dante's *Inferno*."

"Or from the region of the Inquisition's tortures."

"The really pathetic figure is Schindler. What he doesn't endure from the old man! And how devoted he is to him. Like a dog!"

"They say that he has printed on his visiting cards, 'Friend of Beethoven.'"

The laughter grew louder.

VIII

"Dancing was an act of worship,
A sort of praying with the legs."

—HEINE

THE ATTENDANT respectfully ushered Razumovsky to the box of the Thunes and informed him that the intermission was at an end and the symphony about to begin. Almost at the doors Andrey Kirillovitch saw a familiar face. Down the hall came a short man with a happy, good-natured countenance, who glided rather than walked. "Who is he? . . . A Frenchman? . . . A Russian?" The man did not resemble a Russian but something in the Prince's memory connected him with Russia. Gradually Razumovsky recognized the opera dancer, Duport, who, some time ago, had thrilled St. Petersburg and Moscow. An unusually jovial smile spread over the face of the dancer, even though he did not recognize Razumovsky at once. He only remembered that he was an important personage and very pleasant. Duport had not danced for a long time, did not heed his diet, and so had become stout. However, his ballet training was still evident in his walk, facial expression and manner. He even spoke so that the words and thoughts seemed to dance gracefully. When Duport was the topic of conversation ladies invariably said, "Oh, you should have seen him ten years ago!" He greeted Razumovsky warmly.

Without a word they embraced each other. (The attendant looked at them in surprise.) In Russia Andrey Kirillovitch would not have thought of embracing a dancer, even the most famous in the world. But here, in Vienna, Duport was especially dear to him.

"What are you doing here?" inquired Razumovsky. Judging from the surprised expression on the Frenchman's face he surmised that his question did not strike a responsive chord. "Why, don't you know, Prince, that I am manager of the theater?"

"Of course, I know . . . what I wanted to say was: Why aren't you back stage?"

"I have nothing to do there this evening. The theater is rented for the concert. Have you been in Vienna long, Prince? Are you in this box? Alone?"

"Alone."

Razumovsky told him how it had happened. The Thunes had not felt like attending the concert with him (he suspected that their failure to

accompany him was a slight reproof for his be-
havior). "You see how anxious I was to get to
your theater? Won't you sit here with me? I feel
rather awkward, alone in the box."

"With the greatest of pleasure, Prince."

Duport opened the door with a ballet gesture,
allowed the Prince to enter and fluttered into the
box. The auditorium was illuminated by flickering
lights. Some of the musicians were already seated
on the stage, wiping the dust from the kettle-
drums and bass viols. Razumovsky could see, at
first glance, that the audience was not too imposing. The Emperor's box was empty. The Prince's
appearance was noticed by some in the theater;
people bowed to him with joy from all directions.
However, there were fewer of his acquaintances
in the audience than usually attended a state performance. Andrey Kirillovitch assumed a comfortable position in his chair and began to converse
with Duport. They recalled mutual friends. Many
had been dead a long time. Duport had not known.
As each was mentioned his good-natured face
automatically depicted extreme sorrow. This expression on Duport's face seemed to have been
borrowed from some ballet: "The Sultan learns of
his concubine's death," mused the Prince.

"And how is Mademoiselle George?" asked
Razumovsky, smiling.

At one time Duport had had an affair with an eminent actress which had aroused a keen interest among the ladies of Moscow. Now the romance belonged to history and one could discuss it freely. The dancer did not, however, respond without deliberation. His face assumed an expression of extreme modesty. ("Alcide will not betray Galatea's secret.")

"I remember. She kidnapped you in Paris, and brought you in disguise to St. Petersburg. . . . And she did a good thing . . ." said Razumovsky, laughing.

"What a woman! What a woman!" said Duport, widening his eyes. His modesty disappeared before Razumovsky's immodest persistence. ("Alcide *will* betray Galatea's secret.") "The Emperor said she had vulgar extremities. But it's not true, I swear! Her feet are on the large side, perhaps, but what a beauty! . . ."

"I certainly believe you," remarked Razumovsky, smilingly. Andrey Kirillovitch knew this to be the principal conceit in Duport's life. He and Napoleon had been intimate with the same woman. "Yes, those were happy days." With an automatic sigh Duport spoke the automatic phrase. He had made a fortune in Russia. "Those were happy days."

"You are, thank Heaven, well off in Vienna. . . . Are you writing anything now?"

"I am writing a ballet, 'Le Volage Fixe,' "
answered the flattered Duport and began to talk
about his work. Andrey Kirillovitch was envious.
He was jealous of all who had a vocation, and
Duport was genuinely in love with his art. He
talked as if his creative power left him not a minute of leisure. He might be content to drop it all
and begin the life of an ordinary human, but what
about his public? They will not let him alone but
continue their worship. He had retained this tone
since his best years. It even became amplified,
somewhat, when the ladies would say, "Ah, you
should have seen him ten years ago! . . ." Razumovsky listened to him absent-mindedly, studying
the audience, agreeing, or re-questioning him—at
times unapropos.

The theater was beginning to fill. A bell had
sounded in the lobby. The audience was being
seated. The first few rows remained empty, which
fact provoked an unpleasant feeling in Andrey
Kirillovitch. Those empty seats were an insult to
Beethoven and spoiled the appearance of the hall,
as well as the spirits of the assemblage.

"Very, very interesting," the Prince said absent-
mindedly, realizing that he had not said a word
for a long time.

"What is interesting, Prince?"

"What you were saying. . . . But of all your
ballets I prefer that . . . what do you call it . . .

'Galatea.' Tell me, why is there no one in the Emperor's box?"

"His Majesty is not in the city," said Duport respectfully, bowing his head. "Besides, you know, Beethoven is not in good grace at court."

"How is he, the old Jacobin? They say not very well."

Duport was tapping his forehead with his finger and began to speak, this time without ballet gestures: he discussed finances normally.

"Now, Prince," he said, "the capacity receipts of my theater, at the usual prices, amount to twenty-four hundred florins. I reduced the rental fee for the old man as much as I could, because I like him. Yes, I've a weakness for him. . . . They say he *decomposes* music, but I believe he's a good musician, crazy as he is," Duport said with force, as though Razumovsky were contradicting him. "I charged him only one thousand for everything! That is almost at a loss. But the copying of the music alone stood him eight hundred florins! What could one expect at the usual price of admission?"

"With increased prices there would be, perhaps, less of an audience."

"Listen to this: an orchestra was not sufficient. He had to have a choir. Then—soloists. Not one, mind you, four. And how particular he was in

picking them. No ordinary songsters. Henrietta
Sontag he demanded! It's fortunate that she is
such a darling. A gem," added Duport, winking at
Razumovsky. "She doesn't charge him anything.
And such altercations! Had I known it all in ad-
vance I would never have rented my theater to
him. For the baritone part he was offered Forti, a
wonderful singer. 'Nein,' " mimicked Duport, making a ferocious face. "I don't want Forti! *Italien-
ische Gurgelei!*" [1] he exclaimed, pronouncing the
German words with great difficulty but reproduc-
ing Beethoven's voice, manner of speech and
facial expression perfectly. Razumovsky could not
help laughing.

"Yes, he is a stern man."

"That is not all. This little Fräulein Sontag. She
is an angel, Prince. I certainly advise you to pay
especial attention to her." He winked again. "Sontag beseeched him to lower her part—just a little.
What he demands from the singers is terrific! It
sounded reasonable. Why not grant her request and
lower her part? 'Nein!' " still more ferociously bel-
lowed Duport. "Forever '*nein.*' He scolded the
conductor so that the poor fellow was on the point
of refusing to conduct today."

"Why doesn't Beethoven conduct personally?"

Duport looked at Razumovsky, surprised.

[1] Italian gargling.

"For goodness sake, Prince, he is stone deaf. He will be with the director at the music stand. You probably did not see the program. Here. . . ." He took a piece of paper from his pocket. Razumovsky put on his glasses and read the program with interest.

"So it is written to the words of Schiller's 'Ode to Joy,' " drawled Andrey Kirillovitch. He had expected something entirely different from Beethoven. "What joy has he discovered?" thought Razumovsky, with slight anxiety. "This is an old idea of his."

"Yes, poetry. It would be much better to compose music for some good ballet. . . . All the same, ballet is the highest art, because it embodies all other forms of art. I suggested it to him, but all he did was to curse," Dupont again tapped his forehead energetically.

The bell in the lobby rang out louder.

"At last they are commencing. . . . Well, au revoir, Prince. I must leave you. . . . I shall hope to see you in the theater again. I'll drop in here."

He fluttered away, skipping over the threshold of the box. Some tardy musicians were hurrying onto the stage.

Stagehands placed four velvet chairs near the conductor's stand, evidently for the soloists. Others were given ordinary chairs. Schupanzig, Razu-

movsky's old acquaintance, looked out from behind the scenes and disappeared instantly. Attendants were closing the doors. The sound of
tuning up evoked emotion in Razumovsky, re-
calling to his mind something joyous and far, far
away. The lamp-lighters were putting out the
lights. On the walls quivered the reflections of the
candles over the music stands The tardy fire-chief
checked the water level in the brass reservoir on
the stage. Cautious people cleared their throats
ahead of time. The rumble of voices was subsid-
ing.

IX

Vienna, Vienna, city of song,
The lovely city beside the Danube....
— FROM AN OLD SONG

O N THE DAY of the concert, nineteen-
year-old Henrietta Sontag was at a banquet, given in her honor by a young
Hungarian magnate at his country hunting lodge.
Everything at the banquet seemed to have been
copied from a fairy tale: the mysterious castle in
the woods, the spacious low-ceilinged hall decorated with the heads of various animals, a table
that sparkled with crystal and gold, numberless
servants in brilliant costumes, the handsome host
with his curved saber studded with diamonds,
dashing young men, whom he introduced to her,
their impressive names and unusual titles: only in
fairy tales were there princes, marquises, counts,
palatines. In transports of delight these people
were making charming speeches about her talent,
her voice, her beauty.

Lackeys served champagne. She pleaded that

one must not drink before a concert, that she would lose her voice, that she would be hissed at, and, with a weak happy laughter, drank.

Then she sang Rosina's aria and her voice sounded as it had never sounded before.

Resplendent young men fell on their knees, covering her hands with kisses. The host implored her to make him most happy by accepting a modest gift, most unworthy of her divine genius. Taking from a jewel box an exquisite necklace, he placed on her neck the four strands of pearls, touching her bare shoulders with his burning hands as he adjusted the ornament.

She drank, ate sweets, sandwiches after sweets, laughed—half in a dream—happy—mumbled her gratitude—half aware—happy—and stared at those amazing, marvelous people with childish tenderness.

Much later, they thought of the concert. It was necessary to go to the city. The fairy tale continued. She did not know, as yet, that all this was almost a ritual. The young men spread a rug at the portico, before the carriage, so the dust would not touch the feet of their goddess. As another heavy rug was stretched tightly over the bottom stairs, it was impossible to go down them. She laughed, tripped and slid down the stairway. She was caught by the arms, picked up and helped to the carriage. In ecstasy the young men suggested un-harnessing the horses and harnessing themselves in their stead. She protested that this would be impossible as it would bring her too late to the concert. Everyone rocked with laughter and again kissed her hand. The host was anxious to accompany her but forewent that pleasure. It was not in good taste for them to arrive at the theater together.

Henrietta was frightened when the horses sped through the forest. "Supposing bandits attack!" Anything was possible in an enchanted forest.

Despite the spring weather she felt cold. She wrapped a shawl around her throat, counting the first strand of pearls but on her left shoulder, under the shawl, she blissfully lost count. Then she remembered a magnificent phrase which she was to sing at the concert. She tried it with her voice, *"Freude, schoener Goetter Funken, Tochter aus Elysium."* The lackey and coachman turned around from their coachbox. It was impossible to sing loud. The phrase sang soundlessly in her soul. She did not know what "Elysium" was or why a spark was mentioned. Her consciousness did not even take in the words but their melody expressed what she felt on this happiest day of her life. She was thinking of a crazy old man who had written an incomparable symphony, a work of genius, which was to be played this evening for the first time. Herself, this evening's banquet, the pearl necklace, he was glorifying all these, she thought, in this phrase.

Then she fell asleep.

The coachman halted the horses on the square, at the bastion, in front of the impressive Royal Theater.

She awakened and quivered with fright. "Here is the theater and presently I must sing. What if it should be a failure. No. Impossible! Nothing bad can happen. Everything will be marvelous." She stepped lightly from the carriage, somewhat disappointed that no one spread a rug before her, and ran up the steps of the artists' entrance. She was assigned a small dressing room at the end of the hall. Suddenly, through the door which led to the hall, she perceived Beethoven! She stood in the doorway dumfounded.

No one else was in the room. Beethoven sat in a chair with his head on his chest. His face reflected gloom. His eyes, despair. She felt overwhelming compassion for the old man. "How unhappy he must be," she thought, and suddenly, noiselessly stepping into the room, she dropped on her knees before his chair and kissed the hand of Beethoven.

X

++

Beethoven's choral symphony is not entirely devoid of ideas, but they are badly arranged and form an incoherent whole, without charm.

—from an anonymous article of 1831

T HE PERFORMANCE was not an outstandingly grand affair, but all Vienna's connoisseurs of music were in the theater at the Corinthian Gate. The city was full of fantastic rumors concerning Beethoven's new symphony. The old man was beloved by such whimsical admirers as Razumovsky, who cared nothing about the fashion. However, both Schindler and Schupanzig were perplexedly asking themselves what the old man wished to convey this time. Members of the orchestra, who knew their business, looked at each other in amazement. Others, remembering that Weber, after Beethoven's Seventh Symphony, had said that the old man was ripe for the insane asylum, whispered anxiously to one another. The old man's appearance bore out this presumption. At the rehearsals, standing near the conductor, Beethoven stared at the performers with crazed eyes, now shouting, then mumbling incoherently.

Everyone looked at him in astonishment. At the close of the intermission Schindler received the final account of the box-office receipts. He paled as he glanced over the figures. Gross receipts amounted to two thousand two hundred and twenty gulden. Beethoven's share therefore would be a negligible sum of money. And this concert had been his supreme hope.

Schindler knew that he would bear the blame. This did not worry him—he was accustomed to such things. But how could he tell the old man the truth? How would one prepare him? The aged musician had been greatly depressed of late anyway.

Schindler was a literary abstraction. He might have come into the world out of the pages of a sentimental novel, the devoted friend who lived with a great man. He was not playing a part—he probably had never read a novel. He knew music and sincerely worshiped Beethoven. However, had fate not brought them together, he would have become a faithful servant to some other great man. His duties were hard and thankless. Because of that they suited Schindler perfectly. All his life his face bore a melancholy expression. Invariably he was talked of as being devoted to Beethoven, as devoted as a dog, and this was true.

The day of the concert Schindler spent with Beethoven. He ordered the cook to serve the old man's favorite dishes—herring with baked potatoes, an omelet with onions and salami, macaroni and parmesan cheese and a bottle of red Baden wine. He personally prepared the coffee, painstakingly counting exactly sixty beans to the cup, just as Beethoven demanded. The dinner was a success. The old man censured neither Schindler nor the cook, did not throw any plates, and even mumbled in Schindler's direction something that sounded like gratitude for his solicitude. Schindler was at the peak of happiness. Two hours before the concert he took from the wardrobe a green frock-coat (the old man did not own a black one), brushed it and concealing his heartache remarked that in the evening light the green dresscoat, in fact a dark green, undoubtedly would appear black. The concert drew near; Beethoven still sat at the piano. Schindler was becoming anxious. The theater was far away and it would be well to rest before the concert. However, he did not feel he could tear him away from his playing. Schindler sat on the sofa and listened. Beethoven was improvising. His transitional melodies had nothing in common with the theme of the symphony which was to be played at the theater that evening. Schindler knew that it no longer interested Beethoven and concluded that he was playing from his new symphony, the Tenth. It was difficult to follow Beethoven, ever jumping from one theme to another. "Does he hear what he is playing?" Schindler asked himself for the hundredth time and decided as usual that the old man did not hear (orchestral music was inaudible to him within a few paces)—yet he *heard* in some unknown way.

"This is the time an artist should draw him," thought Schindler, as he looked at Beethoven. He felt before him an unknown, unreachable entity.

"How right he is when he says that in art he is nearer to God than all other people!" Having taken counsel with Schupanzig, Schindler decided not to report to the old man the monetary results of the concert. By the general feeling in the auditorium at the beginning of the concert both knew the reception would be warm and Beethoven was assured an ovation. The audience felt sorry for him, being aware of the fact that he had not long to live. Schindler and Schupanzig came timidly into the artists' room. The old man was in the same position in which Sontag had found him.

"Master, pull yourself together," cried Schindler, bending to Beethoven's ear. The contrast between the soft words and the wild shouting was so great that Schindler shuddered. Beethoven rose heavily from his chair and stared in a frenzy at the man who had entered.

"I am roasted, stewed and baked," he said and quickly went in the direction of the stage. Schupanzig followed him with short steps.

XI

✚✚

The Tenth Symphony especially aroused my curiosity since, according to the general opinion of musicians, Beethoven had written it in a condition near to insanity. The symphony was considered the ultimate in incomprehensible and fantastic art. Having procured the score, with great difficulty, I was charmed, at first glance, by its terrible force. Undoubtedly this symphony contained the mystery of mysteries. I remember, the pale light of dawn found me at work. In my condition of utmost excitement, the sunrise frightened me like a ghost. I screamed in terror and covered my face with the blanket.

—FROM RICHARD WAGNER'S REMINISCENCES
OF HIS YOUTH

ON THE other side of the program, in small type, was printed in its entirety, Schiller's "Ode." Andrey Kirillovitch read it slowly. "The verse is not superior, though it *is* Schiller's," he thought. His criticism, however, was directed more to the inner thought of the verse than to its form. The style was rather bold and really cheered one's soul. Razumovsky was far from being in a cheerful mood. His conversation with Duport had aroused melancholy in him, a bitter-sarcastic frame of mind. The verses spoke of a loved woman. Andrey Kirillovitch was in his eighth decade. They spoke of friends and friendship. He had no close friends. "Hm. Why jolly fellows!" he mumbled. "Everything is happiness. All is happiness. 'On the sunlit heights of Faith her banners are seen fluttering.' That's odd. I don't see any banners," thought Razumovsky, changing in his thoughts to French, which was more suitable for irony. " 'Through the chinks in burst coffins Joy may be glimpsed amid a choir of angels.' Now that's something, Joy glimpsed through the chinks in a coffin! 'The gods cannot be requited; it is wonderful to be as they are.' " Andrey Kirillovitch did not at all feel the equal of the gods. "I can't manage that . . . 'May the ledger that records our debts be destroyed . . .' Yes to that! I have several million of those. 'Judge others, as ye are judged by God.' Is the Divine justice to be no better than our own! 'Joy bubbles in the goblet, in the wine's golden blood. Cannibals are drinking tenderness . . .' Even cannibals are at it! No, German poetry and I certainly don't hit it off." A burst of applause interrupted Razumovsky's train of thought. Beethoven was coming out on the stage. "Good Lord! How he has changed." The conduc-

tor, bowing low to the audience, took his place.
Beethoven nodded, turned angrily, and stood
alongside the conductor. The rumble in the
theater ceased entirely. At the first strains of the
music the sarcastic mood left Andrey Kirillovitch.
"What is it?" he thought. "So this is happiness.
. . . But it is not the music he decomposes—it is
life itself. . . . Yes, it is chaos. Darkness and
desolation, the triumph of death."

.   .   .   .   .

"Did you like it, Prince?" asked Duport, who
fluttered into the box as soon as the orchestra
ceased playing. "It was really good, wasn't it?"

He looked with surprise at Razumovsky's weary
face.

"In my opinion, the theme of the finale would
be very appropriate for a ballet. There is a very
similar phrase in a beautiful, ancient Grossvater
dance. A charming phrase."

"For happiness I shall turn to the *Barber of
Seville,*" said Razumovsky after hesitation. He
arose and sat down again. "Let us wait until the
crowd empties into the lobby," he said absent-
mindedly, evidently deep in thought.

"Experts say that all the rules of music are violated in this symphony. You don't think so,
Prince?"

"No. I don't think so. And if they were violated

you have nothing to worry about. It means that he has created new ones," replied Andrey Kirillovitch. He felt the need of expressing his thoughts about the symphony but Duport obviously was the wrong listener.

"So you claim that this is happiness?" said Razumovsky. "I don't know. Never in my life have I heard anything more gloomy and frightful than the first two movements of the symphony. The second movement, in addition, is a mocking one. It is a triumph of evil, an offense, a crime, anything you like but happiness. No, this music is devilish!"

"Why devilish?" incredulously asked Duport. "It seems that happiness enters later. So, at least . . ."

"I don't know when it enters," Razumovsky interrupted. "Not in the third movement. True? Then in the finale? That phrase that reminds you of a Grossvater dance; at that point one's heart is torn out. You say finale," he continued, more intensely. "Why did Beethoven introduce the choir? Even here the man ruins everything. But let us imagine happiness. Did he, in the finale, make answer to the first two movements? To everything that they contain? It is very possible that Beethoven wanted to justify life. He justified nothing. Nothing!"

"I don't understand," Duport replied, still unconvinced. "When the author announces that he will compose happiness, that means he will compose happiness. How can you know better than the composer what he wanted to say? But then at this point he does not philosophize, you see! I know him," he added, shrugging his shoulders.

"Why should he be a philosopher? Beethoven is an enigma. Aren't the methods employed in this composition childish? It's a roll-call of themes. One theme is more divine than another. In the fact that the themes are alternately offered and rejected, also in the quoting of Schiller, there is something naïve and helpless. If you like, only a hair's breadth saves the symphony from banality, yet, after all, Beethoven is the greatest artist of all time—the master of an art that is wiser than all the sages and philosophers in the world. And his pessimism does not come from his consciousness of life's adversities, not even from his deafness. Beethoven is possessed. He creates around himself an atmosphere of torment, then consoles himself as well as he can. On the utmost heights of art voluntary sufferers are needed. Is it possible to create a composition like this in a normal state? What would he do if he justified . . ."

Razumovsky with a guilty feeling looked at Duport. His own words seemed to Andrey Kirillovitch misplaced, not expressing the real thought.

"Perhaps I'm wrong," he said hurriedly, rising. "One understands music as he wishes to."

"Certainly," Duport replied, suppressing a yawn. "Will you go to see him? I don't advise it. He must be very upset. Poor old man. But the artistic success was great. The audience was delighted."

The audience was indeed delighted. As soon as the conductor put down his baton applause thundered. Beethoven did not hear it. He stood motionless, with his back to the audience, holding his hands high in the air. Caroline Unger, a soloist, gently touched his shoulder and, with a smile, pointed in the direction of the applauding audience. His face distorted, he bowed pitifully, and walked toward the exit. The audience did not know that he was totally deaf. The applause ceased abruptly. A spontaneous sigh filled the hall. Then a stormy ovation broke out.

XII

Monsieur Beethoven is small and stocky and his manner is very rude.

—CAMILLE PLEYEL

THE RESULT was even worse than Schindler had imagined. The old man broke out in abuse. He shouted, at the top of his lungs, that the box-office report was inaccurate, that he had been robbed, and let them know, in no uncertain tones, that in his opinion Schindler was a crook though he pretended to be a loyal friend.

Schindler listened humbly to the abuse. It never occurred to him to be offended. Beethoven could do anything—that's why he was Beethoven. Besides, Schindler understood everything perfectly: the old man knew that he was *not* a thief, that he had not robbed him and that he was as loyal as a dog. Beethoven certainly did not believe his own words and, in general, hardly thought of money. In fact he did not need money for himself, but for a youngster, his nephew. He

103

was only pouring out his tortured soul. Schindler understood everything—the old man was not mean, in fact he was by nature very kind—yet there was no more unfortunate man in the world: a pauper, deaf, a zealot of an art which had never satisfied him and which was too superior, too incomprehensible for the public, who applauded only out of a feeling of compassion!

Beseeching the old man to calm himself, trying in every way to describe and amplify the artistic success of the symphony, Schindler, with another friend, Huttenbranner, saw Beethoven home and persuaded him to take a nap. The old man threw himself on the couch and soon fell asleep. Schindler left the room, put out the candles and closed the door behind him.

Next morning, when Schindler came in for a minute to visit Beethoven, he found him there, on the couch. He was still asleep and the old man's face wore the same expression of endless fatigue and torment.

XIII

✛✛

Queens have only one duty: to be beautiful.

—TALLEYRAND

THE CONDUCTOR of the omnibus "The White Lady" pulled the bell-cord and cheerfully, in a shrill voice, sang out something that sounded like the word "*Concord.*"

No passengers arose, except a gentleman wearing glasses, who occupied the first seat of the omnibus' upper deck, near the stairs. He shuddered, arose heavily, leaning upon a cane, and, clutching the rail with his hand in a straw-colored glove, carefully put his foot on the step. The conductor was about to sing out: "*Allons, Messieurs, Dames, dépêchons,*" but changed his mind—the gentleman was evidently very old. Stepping out with the same foot, he hurried down the stairs. The conductor thought that such an old man should never ride on the upper deck: it was both windy and comparatively easy to trip. Two ladies who were standing on the platform moved aside, clearing the way. The gentleman glanced at them, smiled pleasantly—and quite adroitly crossed the platform, not even touching the ladies' crinolines. The conductor had bent his arm in order to help him descend, but stopped, dumfounded; a policeman, at attention, pierced the conductor with a cutting glance, then shifted his eyes towards a light carriage drawn by two beautiful chestnut horses. The carriage was forced to slow down as the omnibus blocked the road. A lady on the platform grew excited: "Look, the Empress!" "The Empress Eugénie!" whispered the other lady, also excited. Everyone at the windows of the omnibus got up, filled with curiosity. The conductor snatched off his cap.

The old gentleman tipped his hat and respectfully bowed to the Empress. She nodded in return and, with a smile, called him over, ordering the coachman to stop.

"*Bonjour, cher Monsieur Isabey,*" she said. The horses moved, and the omnibus rattled on along the pavement. The little girl who sat near the Empress Eugénie, the lackey in his dark-blue livery who held a basket in his hands, the coachman and the policeman gazed with amazement at the stooped old man with his reddish-gray hair, on whose account the Empress had ordered her carriage stopped.

"I am very happy about our meeting. How is your health?"

"I thank you most respectfully, Your Majesty. My health is so good that, upon my word, I am ashamed. I am, Your Majesty almost ninety."

"No one would believe you to be more than sixty."

Monsieur Isabey smiled, realizing that to this woman, so young, about to begin life, sixty and ninety were the same.

"This is my niece," said the Empress, "the daughter of my sister, the Duchess of Alba. My child, this is our celebrated artist, Monsieur Isabey."

The girl, embarrassed, lisped something in Spanish.

"We must speak French," said the Empress sternly. "I want her to be able to say all her life that she saw Isabey with her own eyes," she added with a smile.

Although these words reminded him, indirectly, that he had not much longer to live, Monsieur Isabey appreciated her kindness and it moved him. So close, under a bright sun, he admired the Empress even more than in the palace, where he had seen her at receptions. Her face, her blue eyes, expressed that which had especially moved him in young women: the reflection of happiness, trust and joy of life. "What a beauty," he thought. "I've never seen such hair: neither light nor ash-colored—there is no such color. And what eyes!

One needs only to elongate the oval of her face and it would be impossible to imagine a woman more beautiful." As a connoisseur, he appreciated the Empress' Palmire dress. Her hat matched perfectly the unusual color of her hair. "It seems she does not even wear a hair pad. She herself set the style and has no use for it. . . ."

"Why haven't you visited us for so long?" asked the Empress. Evidently she was seeking a topic of conversation. Having detained the old man, she felt obliged to converse with him another minute or two. "The Emperor is always glad to see you. I should like your advice about my portrait. Who, in your opinion, is better: Winterhalter or Dubuff?"

"Both are splendid artists, Your Majesty," promptly replied Monsieur Isabey.

"What a pity that you don't choose to paint me! I wish you . . ."

"For goodness' sake, don't make fun of an old man, Your Majesty," Monsieur Isabey said with a sigh. "I haven't painted for a long time—I choose not to disgrace myself: the brush trembles in my hand."

"I am confident that even now you can paint better than any young artist. Now, do call on us, simply, without ceremony. The Emperor intends to consult you about the court ceremonial. We

wish it to be identical with that of our late uncle
and no one except you saw it . . ." she said and
suddenly blushed. Monsieur Isabey smiled affably. It was amusing to hear this young Spanish
Countess—who, practically unknown until a short
time ago, through a miracle had become the
Empress of France—call Napoleon I her uncle.
But the fact that she, herself, had become confused and blushed touched him.

"I am at the service of Your Majesty."

"What a fortunate man you are, Monsieur
Isabey. You knew our uncle, painted his portrait."

"Your Majesty, allow me to remind you," said
Monsieur Isabey with a smile, "I did not paint
only your uncle. A long time before that I also
painted your most august grandmother."

"My grandmother?" perplexedly inquired the
Empress.

"The late Queen Marie Antoinette," explained
Monsieur Isabey. "Your uncle's wife, Empress
Marie Louise, was related to Queen Marie An-
toinette."

The Empress looked at Monsieur Isabey, puz-
zled. His smile was so pleasant and respectful
that there could be no question of irony. But at
the thought that this very man had sketched the
Queen who had been executed more than sixty

years previously, on this very square, the Empress felt frightened. She decided that one should not, that it was not proper for one to live so long.

Hastily dismissing Monsieur Isabey, she ordered the coachman to drive on.

XIV

*The abundance of grace which God was pleased to grant
me, and the peace with which He filled me were so great
that I could hardly refrain from laughing all the time.*
                                    —CLAUDE LANCELOT

"IF ONLY she, too, does not meet with misfortune," thought Monsieur Isabey, remembering what he had seen in his time. But
he cast aside all sad presuppositions and trans-
ferred his thoughts to his original purpose: he
was on his way to eat oysters. He dined after
the old manner, at five o'clock, and lunched at
noon—more often at home, but occasionally in
restaurants, whenever it was possible to leave
his wife. Monsieur Isabey, a splendid husband,
was very much in love with his second wife—as
he had been with his first—however, he was not
averse to diverting himself occasionally without
her. He stopped at the delicatessen shop. Monsieur Isabey liked to examine showcases. In a
large box with low sides there lay a pineapple,
encircled with pears—not unlike a king-pin sur-

rounded by bowling pins. Beside it, in jelly, there
was an enormous dish of goose-liver paste,
studded with black truffles. In the back, towering
over jars of preserves, gherkins, sardines, protruded various bottles with silver, blue and red
necks—one more beautiful than the other. Monsieur Isabey walked on quickly. His appetite had
increased.

At the sight of the goose-liver paste he recalled
that the Empress' lackey had held a basket in
his hands. "Probably visiting the poor again, in-
cognita," thought Monsieur Isabey good-naturedly.

From his friend, Fould, who held the position
of Minister of the Court, he had learned how the
police arranged the Empress' charity trips. Fould,
a very jolly man, described them humorously to
a few intimate friends. The coachman would
bring the young Empress to a poor house in a
poor district. The lackey remained below, while
the Empress, with a basket in her arms, mounted
the narrow but spotlessly clean stairway—into a
mansard-attic occupied by destitute people. Incidentally, the Prefect of Police usually chose a
house not too tall and with a fairly slanting stairway.

A neatly dressed little boy invariably answered
the knock at the door and stared at the visitors,

his eyes red with weeping. A cough was heard from the far end of the attic; an ill woman with a kind, sad and emaciated face, rising heavily from the bed, asked in a weak voice: "Who is there?" The Empress then came near the bed and explained to the woman that the Brotherhood of St. Vincent had delegated her to call on the sick widow. The widow, full of emotion, thanked her and related the circumstances in a weak, broken voice. "Indeed, we live very, very poorly. Of course, no one is at fault. We are all well off with the kind Emperor Napoleon who loves his people so dearly. In my household one misfortune follows another. My beloved husband died, I am sick, but what can one do? I am not thinking of myself —but how shall I feed this poor, hungry child?" Tears rolled from the widow's eyes. The Empress, having shed a few tears, took from the basket a Strasbourg pie, a fat chicken, some large pears and port wine. "The Brotherhood sends you this," the Empress said. The boy, crying with delight, ate greedily, the widow sobbed tears of emotion. "But you! Who are you, our angel, our Providence?" she cried, covering the Empress' hands with kisses. "Mother, mother, look!" shouted the boy. "Why, this beautiful lady resembles very closely our kind Empress! . . ." The widow then looked at the Empress with eyes wide with awe

and happiness. The Empress wiping away her
tears stepped out from the attic leaving behind
her on the table a knitted purse with gold coins.

The Minister of the Court and the Prefect of
Police knew many variations on these charity trips.
Monsieur Isabey listened to Fould, not without
pleasure—there was nothing wrong in it and no
one was harmed. "She, the poor thing, is gratified
to know how they are loved by their people. For
that reason, 'one must speak French,'" thought
Monsieur Isabey, smiling kindly.

At the café, on both sides of the door, one on
top of the other, were piled wicker baskets filled
with oysters and snails. Monsieur Isabey stopped
at the display, scrutinizing the baskets through
his glasses. "Supposing I order a dozen of each?"
he asked himself, thoughtfully. "I oughtn't to."
However, he immediately answered himself. Perhaps he had only a few days to live—it would
be too bad not to have enjoyed the oysters—for
the last time. Though he was not superstitious,
in any event, he tapped his cane with the thin,
bony, middle finger of his left hand. "It couldn't
injure one's health." The woman behind the
counter looked at him disapprovingly, thinking
it improper for an old man who had already outlived his welcome in this world to be viewing
the display, that his grandchildren were commit-
ting a sin by letting him wander alone in the

streets. Monsieur Isabey entered the café and selected a comfortable place. The waiter moved his table and took his order, his thoughts the same as the woman's behind the counter.

"And what will you drink? I have English beer," said the waiter.

Monsieur Isabey only looked at him. He knew that this was the latest vogue brought in by the English: after oysters to drink beer, not wine. But Monsieur Isabey regarded the gastronomical tastes of the English with contempt. He examined the wine list carefully. There was the rare vintage of 1846 but, without stars, meaning there were no pints. To order a whole bottle was too expensive and imprudent. But Monsieur Isabey again thought that perhaps it was the last time in his life he would lunch in this fashion. Summoning the waiter by rapping on the back of the couch, he ordered a whole bottle of wine.

Monsieur Isabey relished the oysters, using neither lemon juice nor sauce—these also were foolish novelties and only spoiled the flavor of the oysters. Intermittently thinking about the oysters he thought also of various other things. "Fould undoubtedly can arrange Henrietta's affairs. It would be well to find a prospective husband in his immediate family. The differences in religion matter little. Each would remain loyal to his own. The oysters are fine. What a beautiful woman the Empress is! God bless her. I must call on them at the Tuilleries."

Monsieur Isabey had frequented the Court at the time of Louis XVI, Napoleon I, Louis XVIII, again at the time of Napoleon, Charles X, Louis-Philippe: no one stayed at the palace long and it brought them all misfortune. "Perhaps it will not bring them ill luck," optimistically thought Monsieur Isabey. "And if it does, what can one do? It is impossible to live one's whole life without misfortune." Deep in his heart he did not believe this: one might live a whole life without any misfortune.

Monsieur Isabey grew heavy from the oysters and wine. He felt like taking a nap. He had always resisted this sign of old age and decided to return home on foot: the weather was beautiful. Drinking the remaining wine, he paid his bill, nodded to the waiter, and left the café—a little more bent and leaning heavily on his cane. The waiter was shaking his head, winking to the other patrons. The woman at the counter, who had watched, through the window, how Monsieur Isabey was faring, looked at him with a combination of horror and admiration. "I hope he won't go in for a girl as well, that decrepit old man," she said to herself.

XV

✤✤✤

Who thinks of death, is already half dead.

— HEINE

THE DAY was wonderful. Monsieur Isabey did not feel like returning home.
"Perhaps I should go to see the latest
'Delaroche'?" he thought. Monsieur Isabey attended exhibitions regularly: he had grown tired
of the war between the romanticists and classicists; moreover he was not able to understand the
difference bettween classicists and romanticists.
Monsieur Isabey judged painters by only one cri-
terion: some knew their craft, others didn't. Before, at the beginning of this endless war, Monsieur
Isabey had sincerely desired to know what it
was all about, curious as to which he was, a classicist or a romanticist. But he realized, with concern, that young artists did not ask themselves
this question—they could not even analyze it:
Monsieur Isabey represented the past, which was
uninteresting as a subject for discussion—just as
most ardent politicians would not be interested

117

in Merovingians and Carlovingians. Monsieur
Isabey did not feel hurt. The young artists amused
him a little, especially the romanticists—those who
painted less well than the classicists but knew a
bit more.

Locusta was poisoning a slave before the eyes
of laughing Nero. With guffaws, ferocious Turks
butchered defenseless women and children. A
wild steed galloped with Mazzepa tied to its tail.
Charles I was being insulted by Cromwell's sol-
diers. Heliogabalus was throwing his guests to
tigers to be devoured. Saul's wife was driving
away a buzzard from the dead bodies of her
hanged sons. "What ridiculous people. Where do
they find such subjects?" thought Monsieur
Isabey, who in all his life had never seen a host
who threw his guests to tigers to be devoured nor
a mother who drove away a buzzard from the
corpses of her hanged sons. "It couldn't be so. And
if it were, why recall these vile things? And if one
decides to recall them, he should know his subject.
Someone reads a drama, looks at an album, and
the result—an historical painter."

The reason Monsieur Isabey had such difficulty
in understanding the difference between the classicists and romanticists was the fact that he knew
all of them well, was acquainted with their affairs,
their parents, their wives and mistresses: all these

young people seemed to him so much alike. They all struggled equally hard to attract public atten- tion. "There is no harm in it, but why such violent conflict of parties? Why is Paul, the youngster who yesterday was put in the corner for stealing a pie, a romanticist? Why is that blockhead, George, a classicist?" Monsieur Isabey asked him- self cheerfully as he roamed through the exhibi- tion rooms. His placid bewilderment left him, however, when he viewed the canvases of the leaders of the various schools. He turned away from some pictures with an involuntary sigh. But Monsieur Isabey loved art to such an extent that he immediately cast aside any feeling of jealousy. "Perhaps, some day, they will find a place in the Louvre for me, too," he consoled himself. Enger's passionate hatred of Delacroix was incomprehen- sible to him. "All the same, they will hang side by side in the Museum and every ten years one or the other will be crowned and uncrowned."

Monsieur Isabey changed his mind about at- tending the exhibition. "Perhaps someone else will be strangled or I may encounter another Locusta. I had better not . . ." On this sunny day, after wine and oysters, he wasn't in the mood for look- ing at murderers, even if they were very well painted.

Suddenly remembering that he was expecting

guests that evening, Monsieur Isabey went to the confectioners and ordered tarts, cakes and sandwiches. Then he decided to continue his walk, hoping to meet acquaintances, but was disappointed in that respect. At Lespess', as usual, there was a gathering of elegant ladies. Monsieur Isabey was all attention, comparing the contemporary beauties with those of the past. "Those of the past were more beautiful. But the contemporary ones are not bad."

Near the Institute a shop with a newly painted sign had opened. Not long before, it had been a bookshop, but the owner had failed in business and the shop had remained locked for about two weeks. Monsieur Isabey noticed with displeasure that an undertaker was now established there.

On a black board, silver letters were outlined: "Funeral Parlor." The show window was already decorated: on dark-blue silk there reposed prominently a large maroon coffin. In back of the coffin were metal wreaths leaning against tall iron standards. On either side, in dark frames, lay obituary notes with black borders, dotted lines in the white spaces; it was necessary only to write in the name of the deceased. A notice explained that the management attended to every detail: "Death announcements, purchase of cemetery lots, letters announcing decease." Monsieur Isabey read the notice morosely, as though the owner's solicitude seemed to him somewhat tactless. It was unpleasant to him that in his neighborhood there was a man who made his living from the dead, one who obviously wished for the speedy death of his neighbors. "Free advice," read Monsieur Isabey. The kindness of the undertaker decidedly did not impress him. "Never mind, no hurry," he thought, examining the coffin. "Of course, it isn't pleasant, yet I am not afraid." Monsieur Isabey really was not afraid of death and thought of it but seldom. "There can be nothing bad. True, nothing good. It will perhaps be difficult for two or three days. It is a pity, indeed, but I am not afraid. I am about to die and not afraid. . . . Perhaps I may not even die soon. And perhaps the undertaker will manage to fail as his predecessor failed . . ."

Monsieur Isabey turned away from the window somewhat triumphantly, and went on his way.

At the corner, near the café, stood a smoking brazier with chestnuts. Monsieur Isabey was very fond of chestnuts. Their sweet, distinctive flavor brought back his early youth. "Around the corner, on Butcher Street, near the inn, there also was a roast chestnut pedlar. The old coachman used to warm himself at the charcoal fire and tell about the good times under Louis XIV."

Monsieur Isabey recalled something very far away which had happened nearly eighty years previously. "I also have outlived my time and it is well that I have lived too long," he thought, and, bracing himself, as though to spite the undertaker, ordered three sous' worth of chestnuts.

XVI

❖·❖

The important thing in this world is to fight off boredom.
—DELACROIX' MEMOIRS

NOT SO LONG AGO Monsieur Isabey had kept open house, entertaining constantly. People of entirely different points of view, who never met anywhere else, visited Monsieur Isabey, chatted amiably—or at least politely—and, at times, even played cards. Monsieur Isabey's usual attitude at these gatherings, now and then unexpected, expressed in substance this: "All of you, as a matter of fact, are fine people and one is no worse than another; therefore, I adjure you: This is a fine time to stop calling one another scoundrels and idiots; please believe an old man; it is unnecessary and improper. Do what you like, but here in my house, please behave yourselves correctly." This attitude, together with the appearance and character of the host, gave the house of Monsieur Isabey an aspect of exceptional charm, to which the most quarrelsome and irreconcilable people succumbed. Incidentally they forgot it as soon as they reached the street. Once a year Monsieur Isabey organized masquerades which had the reputation of being the gayest in Paris: the guests were entertained by the most celebrated artists, singers and musicians—only at his house was it possible to see and hear them close at hand and free of charge. To a certain extent freedom reigned in this house. Monsieur Isabey, as an artist, but even more as a bit of the Eighteenth Century, pre-served by some miracle, could indulge in more freedom than the rest. He was very partial to young people and enjoyed, in a fatherly way, patronizing lovers. Certain prim acquaintances even claimed that his patronizing of lovers went too far. In the workshop of his old residence Monsieur Isabey had had a couch which was known to all Paris. The head of the couch could be lifted and there a spiral stairway led to the lower floor of the building: in this fashion lovers who were meeting at Monsieur Isabey's under pretense of ordering a portrait, could, in case of necessity, disappear without attracting attention; not by the back stairs but poetically by the con-cealed stairway under the couch.

Now things had changed a great deal. Monsieur Isabey's second wife enjoyed delicate health. He painted no more and in the Institute where, through friendship and connections, he had the use of a splendid residence—without cost—there were no spiral stairways. The couch was nailed up. Now Monsieur Isabey entertained less frequently. The duties of hostess were usually discharged by the young daughter of Monsieur Isabey: she had been born when he was in his seventies—this event had amused Parisians at the time. She was assisted by another pretty young lady who was always there. She was called the pupil of Monsieur Isabey. Her resemblance to him was striking. Those near to him knew how much he loved his girls and how anxious he was to marry them off—the sooner and the more profitably the better—in fact, in his old age, this was his only worry. For these girls he infrequently arranged parties. A husband, of course, could be found without them, but Monsieur Isabey knew that husbands were found more easily if they were looked for. He knew also that love was a great thing, without a doubt the greatest in life, but under secure circumstances, amid gay leisure, love comes more quickly and lasts longer These were the conditions that he was anxious to create for his girls.

His main hope was Fould. The old banker, Behr Fould, who had been his close friend, was dead. But his son, who had become Minister of the Court, the Emperor's favorite, one of the richest men in France, could without difficulty, in Monsieur Isabey's opinion, find a suitable match for Henrietta. Fould was at present in especial grace at the Tuilleries because he was the leader of the so-called "party of marriage for love": the majority of the ministers had advocated a dynastic marriage of the Emperor with some foreign princess. Fould's party had been victorious and the Empress was especially partial to him. Monsieur Isabey was depending upon Fould with whom he had kept up friendly relations: he liked this clever, gay and harmlessly cynical man. Fould was very vain; however, his vanity was so obvious and naïve that it didn't offend Monsieur Isabey. With the advent of old age he was becoming more and more tolerant.

XVII

Among the members of the Senate and of the Cabinet who were summoned to the Elysée to receive certificates of nomination, and to express their gratitude, there was a young man, active, witty and earnest, a veteran Deputy to the National Assembly from Alsace. He had served with the Gardes-Cavaliers of the Russian Emperor, returning to France after a duel which had in many ways excited St. Petersburg society.

—FROM THE MEMOIRS OF
GRANIER DE CASSAGNAC

MONSIEUR ISABEY had a presentiment that the evening would be slow and dull. Ten guests had been invited. A most inconvenient number: too many for a friendly talk and not enough for a reception where guests could entertain themselves. In order to liven things up a bit, Monsieur Isabey had devised a reading: a young novelist had consented to read her latest novel. Though Monsieur Isabey hoped that the novelist would have a lively conscience and read no more than half an hour, he was in doubt, even though on the previous day he had very significantly told the novelist's husband, an architect who was very much in love with her: "I assure you it will be a treat! Twenty minutes of reading! With the talent of the little woman, it will be a rare treat!"

Fould was the most important guest. Although he was no stranger in the house, he nevertheless held the place of honor. Monsieur Isabey knew that even with the son of an old friend one must not become too familiar—especially if the friend's son should become a Minister of the Court. Of Fould it was said that he could accomplish anything. This was felt in the radiant expression of his face. He was neither an impudent nor an arrogant man but, entirely independent of his will, his expression invariably implied: "Yes, I have been successful in everything, but I am just beginning! Perhaps you may succeed too—I might even assist you if it weren't too much trouble." Fould had many enemies.

The other guests were, in the main, young and unimportant: artists, friends of Monsieur Isabey's son, companions of Henrietta, and her music teacher. The position of second importance was held by a beautiful woman, Paiva, about whom gossip in Paris increased from day to day. She

was a marchioness, rich, but it would be difficult
to recognize her as an honored guest if only for
the fact that in many homes she would not be
allowed past the threshold. She was called an ad-
venturess by those hostile to her and, at times,
by a more emphatic name. Her history had, indeed, been turbulent. Paiva, the daughter of
Lachman, a tailor, had been born and bred in
Moscow, roamed through all the capital circles
of the world, had married three times, left three
husbands, been the ruin of several lovers—a
Russian prince, an English lord, two French
dukes—and at present was enjoying life. She evidently cared very little what people in general
and ladies of society in particular said about her.

Characteristically, Paiva, upon finding herself
at Monsieur Isabey's, paid not the slightest attention to the serious and dignified air with which
her hostess greeted her. The Marchioness Paiva
rarely conversed with ladies, and recognized only
the more important gentlemen. This evening, at
Monsieur Isabey's, there were no celebrities present and the Marchioness was visibly bored. Fould
was the only gentleman she singled out from
among the guests: but the Minister of the Court
was not very young. Fould, who had an emotional
weakness for women, lost no time in choosing a
seat next to hers and did not leave her for the

remainder of the evening, entertaining her with
stories about the Emperor.

The girls, Henrietta's friends, with eager curiosity kept their eyes on the lady about whom so
many exciting and mischievous things were being
said. She was gowned sumptuously. In taste, in
richness of dress and jewelry, Paiva rivaled the
Empress: some even asserted that she eclipsed
her.

Monsieur Isabey welcomed the Marchioness
with the utmost courtesy and kindness. He had always defended her, saying that neither the past
of such a beautiful woman nor her manner of
living was anyone's concern. "And she is also
very intelligent," Monsieur Isabey always added
convincingly.

"I was afraid you might be away, at some
country house," he said, with difficulty drawing
a chair towards the Marchioness. Fould glanced
at the old man with slight displeasure.

"At a country house? What an idea! I agree
with dear Auber when he says, 'The country is
good for little birds,' " replied Paiva.

At this moment the last guest entered—the next
in importance to Fould. He was a senator—yet a
young man, according to the newspapers the
youngest of all the senators. He immediately drew
the ladies' attention. Paiva trained her lorgnette

on him and kept it at her eyes for nearly a minute.
He was a handsome man of athletic build dressed
extremely well—in the most fashionable clothes,
exceptionally courteous and fascinating. He was
a Frenchman, but spoke with a slight German
accent. He bore a foreign name—some Dutch
baron had adopted him. Fould whispered to
Paiva that the Emperor was very partial to the
newcomer: after the political change he had been
appointed a member of the Committee of Council, then sent with an important mission to foreign
sovereigns.

With the Senator's arrival the drawing room
became more cheerful. Fould was put in the back-
ground. The young Senator at once enlivened the
conversation, previously so dull, entertaining the
ladies and getting off pleasantries which sounded
much alike. Paiva looked less bored; the novelist
made mental notes of the Senator's appearance,
for future reference in her next novel; the girls
perked up and all the guests felt at once that
this man was meant to be "the life of the party."

Refreshments were being served in the dining
room next to the salon. Not to burden Madame
Isabey, a caterer supplied everything. In these
elder days Monsieur Isabey had become very eco-
nomical and ordered refreshments for only ten,
omitting himself and his wife. The service sup-

plied was second rate—there were no caviar
sandwiches. The young artists glanced anxiously
towards the dining room, speculating as to which
would come first: would they be invited to the
buffet or would the reading commence? A servant
girl, in a Swiss costume, who was helping the
waiter supplied by the caterer, entered the sitting room with a tray which held a decanter of
lemonade and a glass. The young artists understood the ill-omened sign: the reading would
come first. The novelist paled somewhat and suddenly, to the guests' amazement lighted a cigar.
Monsieur Isabey smiled pleasantly: he knew that
this was done in imitation of George Sand. It was
amusing: the novelist, a very fine woman, who
lived with her husband in accord and happiness,
did not resemble George Sand in anything but
the cigar. "The poor woman is defending herself
from society with her cigar as does George with
her sarcastic remarks," thought Monsieur Isabey.
At the sight of the cigar the novelist's husband, a
stout good-natured man wearing glasses, looked
timidly at the host, but was comforted by the
sympathetic smile of Monsieur Isabey, and busied
himself moving the table and candles. "She likes
to read without light on her face." he explained
in a nervous whisper to Monsieur Isabey, who
nodded his head understandingly Paiva was star-

ing at the novelist with a disdainful smile. Fould sighed and made himself comfortable in his chair. The Senator was concluding his story to Mademoiselle Henrietta in a whisper: "Emperor Franz Josef? A very amiable youngster. Later, I shall tell you about the Austrian Court."

From the antechamber the novelist's husband brought an elegant portfolio the thickness of which drew the guests' attention. The folder was a thin one. Monsieur Isabey emitted a sigh of relief. The room became silent. Without opening her manuscript, the novelist said a few words: the subject of the novel had been taken from the period of the Italian Middle Ages, the action taking place in Ravenna during the era of Polentas Vidame.

"Of course the spirit is most important, not the facts," said the novelist. "The spirit of Ravenna and the spirit of the Middle Ages." Suddenly the novelist dropped her cigar case. Her husband dashed forward from his corner but was too late: the Senator, smiling amiably, was already handing the case to the novelist. She thanked him with a smile and, opening the book, began to read. The villain from the period of the Polentas, lords of Ravenna, committed one crime after another: the girls listened horrified—it would be an achievement to enter a dark room, after the reading.

Fould dozed, glancing at the yawning Marchioness once in a while. Monsieur Isabey was nodding his head, fighting drowsiness: at his age he fell asleep easily. The architect in glasses watched the audience emotionally, whispering something in his neighbor's ear but never finishing—not to distract their attention from the reading.

The reading lasted thirty-five minutes. The novelist, after all, had a conscience. Having finished, she closed the portfolio and bowed, smiling pleasantly. There was applause. Monsieur Isabey, bending forward in his chair, kissed the writer's hand and with an enthusiastic smile on his kind old face told her something flattering. Other guests also paid their compliments. Fould demanded that the novel be published as soon as possible and advised applying to the *Revue des Deux Mondes* but was sorry afterwards because the architect immediately requested a letter of recommendation to the editor. Fould promised to recommend it highly but orally.

"The portrayal of the spirit of the Middle Ages was very important to her," explained the architect. "You understand, the spirit . . ."

"And she portrayed it beautifully," agreed the Senator affably.

Then everyone walked into the dining room. The party was rather gay. There was no general conversation but small groups talked animatedly.

"Nevertheless, I should like to know what you meant to convey in your splendid novel," said Monsieur Isabey, concerned, as he handed the novelist a plate with a piece of fruitcake. He felt that she expected a serious debate on the novel.

"It was important to her to express the spirit ..." began the architect but his wife immediately interrupted him.

"I was interested in a perfect villain type, a man without any moral foundation," she said, and blushed. "That is why I plunged into the depths of the Middle Ages."

Monsieur Isabey's face expressed full satisfaction.

"Now I understand."

"That is very interesting," said Fould. "What do you consider the basic indication of crime?"

"Basic indication? Certainly the harm suffered by society."

"Correct," agreed the Senator. "That which harms society is criminal."

Fould argued a while, addressing his remarks largely to Paiva. He was trying to prove that real villains were a thing of the past and would never return. The ladies agreed, with regret. Only Paiva stubbornly remained silent, her smile becoming more and more contemptuous. The novelist's replies were brisk. The architect in glasses beamed with pride. The debate at the buffet lasted about five minutes. In Monsieur Isabey's opinion this was sufficient, especially since there were hardly any sandwiches or pastries on the plates. The guests were ushered back into the sitting room and there broke up into groups. The stiffness of the early evening had disappeared. Fould was again at Paiva's side, conducting an oral attack: he did not like to lose time and did not consider the situation as hopeless. The hostess conversed with the novelist's husband. The girls entertained the Senator. Mademoiselle Henrietta showed him a splendid Daguerre photographic apparatus, her father's birthday present to her. Unexpectedly, Paiva displayed an interest in the apparatus; the Senator lifted and carried it like a feather though it was exceedingly heavy. Mademoiselle timidly explained to the Marchioness the intricacies of the Daguerre apparatus, pulled out from the box a square camera obscura with a collapsible top, an iodine box which could be drawn out, and a receptacle for mercury with a thermometer and an alcohol lamp below. Gathering courage, Henrietta offered to take the Marchioness' picture at some opportune time but Paiva definitely refused.

"It is too tiring," she said. "Why, I understand one must sit motionless for at least twenty minutes."

"Oh, no. If the gown is not white, on a sunny day on the terrace, ten minutes would be entirely sufficient."

"All the same . . . It is beyond my strength."

At the request of the writer, Monsieur Isabey exhibited his collection of miniatures. The guests gathered around him, admiring the beautiful portraits. Monsieur Isabey sighed as he called out the names; all his subjects were dead.

"This is the poor King of Rome . . . This the Duchess Angoulême . . . Princess Volkonsky, a Russian . . . I painted her in Vienna, during the Congress . . . Ah, what a beautiful woman! Really, more beautiful than you!" he said addressing Paiva. Mademoiselle Henrietta was stunned and looked at her father in amazement: but Monsieur Isabey smiled calmly, good-naturedly. He knew that Paiva would not feel insulted. Paiva only smiled proudly.

"This, my dear friend, only seems so because you were then forty years younger," said Fould.

"Very possible . . . This is the Duchess Dino. . . . And this is another Russian, Princess Bagration. She is still alive . . . The Russian ladies are very beautiful . . ." said Monsieur Isabey and faltered. He had suddenly remembered that the Senator, some years ago, had met with a very disagreeable adventure in Russia where he had killed someone in a duel. This combat had given the Baron great prestige with the ladies. Monsieur Isabey decided that it might be better not to discuss Russia. Yet he, himself, had married a Russian and, oddly enough, a relative of the slain man.

The conversation about Russia was not unpleasant to the Baron. He admitted that he had seen many exceptional beauties in St. Petersburg. Having learned that the Senator had lived in Russia for many years, Paiva spoke to him in Russian. But the Baron's knowledge was very meagre.

"Lioubliou . . ." "Otchen krassiva . . ." "Skolko stoit . . ." he burst forth. "I have forgotten it all, Madam, and I regret it. I adore everything Russian."

Fould, smiling amiably towards the influential Senator, told of the important mission which had been fulfilled with great success by the Baron. For this mission he had been given *carte blanche.* Before sending him to Vienna Emperor Napoleon had told him: "You have enough wit and worldly wisdom to get along without further instruction."

The Senator reciprocated by paying the Minister a compliment and described his conversation with the Czar while in Berlin. Then the conversation shifted to Emperor Nicholas, the ladies asking if he was as handsome as his portraits showed him.

"He is an old man now but twenty years ago, when I first saw him, there wasn't a man in the world who could approach his majestic appearance," affirmed the Senator. Politics became the following subject of conversation. Fould said that, unfortunately, a war with Russia was inevitable.

Monsieur Isabey, suddenly growing angry, began arguing that war was not at all inevitable.

"Why should we and the Russians start butchering one another, without any reason?" he demanded bitterly.

Both the Minister and the Senator smiled.

"Prince Menshikoff's trip to Constantinople and Emperor Nicholas' policy made the war, for us, a question of honor," declared Fould.

"I've heard that many times. There are in my memory dozens of wars and all of them were good for nothing. These are the identical words that I used to General Bonaparte," said Monsieur Isabey, provoked. The words "I used to General Bonaparte" had a magical effect on his listeners. All stared at the old man with intense interest, waiting for him to continue.

"Did you really tell General Bonaparte that?" asked Fould, with curiosity.

"Certainly, I told him . . . I remember particularly, I had dined with them at Malmaison. The First Consul came to the table, as gloomy as a cloud: he had just received a communication about the Emperor Paul's assassination. . . . Everyone was whispering that war was inevitable. . . ."

He stopped.

"And the First Consul?"

"The First Consul! He would laugh at any suggestion of mine," replied Monsieur Isabey. All laughed. The Marchioness Paiva asked the host to tell them about Queen Marie Antoinette.

"They say you knew her, but this really is hard to believe."

"Of course, I knew her," affirmed Monsieur Isabey. "I was a young man when I first met her. I was assigned to paint the little nephews of the Queen, the Dukes d'Angoulême and Berry. I was painting in the children's room . . . All of a sudden there was confusion, people bustled about . . . 'The Queen is coming!' I was struck with awe . . . She came in." . . . Monsieur Isabey hesitated. "She was also a beauty."

"Well, what then?"

"She sat near me, watching . . . From that time on I became used to kings and I have seen many of them in my life. But this was the first time . . . And it was different then; we thought of them as gods, not human beings. I painted and trembled . . . She smiled, arose kissed her

nephews and said to me, 'Until we meet, my child.
Your work is nice. . . .' Evidently she liked me:
three days later I was invited to the Trianon to
paint the Queen. From then on, I found myself in
their set. I went to their balls, and dallied around
at Court."

"And then?" asked the architect.

"What, then?" Monsieur Isabey imitated. "Then
the Revolution. You have probably heard? The
Queen was executed. . . ." The guests were filled
with horror, as had been Empress Eugénie that
morning.

"And do you know, ladies and gentlemen," said
the Senator, "we have recently received unfortunate news from Mexico: Countess Rossi died suddenly, of cholera . . ."

"Countess Rossi?" repeated Fould, growing
pale.

"Who is Countess Rossi?" inquired the architect.

"Don't you know? Henrietta Sontag. . . ."

"Impossible!"

Fould was stunned. In his youth he had been
in love with Sontag—and he was terribly afraid
of death.

"From cholera."

The older guests were reminiscing. They remembered the celebrated singer, her beauty, her

triumphs, her rivalry with Malibran, their famous quarrel and their reconciliation.

"You remember the British Ambassador in Berlin offered her his hand. Useless! What *was* his name? I have forgotten."

"A number of men committed suicide on her account."

"It was the King of Prussia who arranged her marriage to young Rossi."

"Yes. And then, the poor thing, she had to yield to her husband and give up the stage . . . In the bloom of youth and talent."

"It is a good thing that Rossi was ruined and she had to return, not so long ago."

"Yes, after twenty years."

"But the public accepted her with the same enthusiasm as before . . ."

"No, hardly with the same. . . . Poor Sontag. She went on tour to America, to die there of cholera."

Fould found himself picturing Henrietta Sontag's death: that goddess in cholera cramps, at a Mexican inn!

The guests continued to talk of Countess Rossi and of other, more recent singers. Madame Isabey insisted that her daughter play the pianoforte: her husband had forgotten the principal object of the reception—it was necessary to show off Henrietta's talent. She played something from Beethoven for four hands, with her music teacher. Her performance was praised. Even the Marchioness Paiva, herself a splendid musician, paid her a compliment. Monsieur Isabey, who had fallen into the mood of reminiscence, was describing his meeting with Beethoven in Vienna, at the Congress.

"He was a very peculiar man. . . . We knew nothing about him in Vienna. But one of our friends, Prince Razumovsky, even then foresaw his eminence."

The music teacher told how Beethoven, during the last days of his life, had been preparing a new composition which, if compared with his former ones, would have dimmed them. He had planned to call it the Tenth Symphony. He intended to pour his whole soul into it. Yet he did not succeed in writing his Tenth Symphony. He only dreamed, and died while dreaming.

"Indeed?" inquired Monsieur Isabey, this time with genuine interest. He sighed and grew thoughtful. "Every one has his Tenth Symphony," he said.

"That's true," Fould agreed, looking at the Marchioness. He had already managed to regain his poise after the sad news. He was anxious to express a deeply felt thought. "In reality, we are all failures."

The guests laughed. So unexpected was this remark from the lips of a man who, during his life, had succeeded in everything. Fould was flattered by the surprise of the guests but he defended his thought. The conversation had assumed a philosophical character. The novelist quoted Goethe. Fould and the Senator were also able to sustain conversation about Goethe.

The guests left at eleven o'clock. They knew that their host, an old man, was not supposed to stay up late. Monsieur Isabey mounted the stairs with a candle in his hand. All the bedrooms in his house were on the second floor. Having washed, he went, in a dark-red silk dressing gown, to his wife's bedroom and visited with her for five minutes, exchanging impressions. His wife thought Paiva was an unpleasant, impudent woman, that it was unnecessary to have invited her.

"Instead of being grateful to decent ladies for inviting her, she holds out only two fingers."

Monsieur Isabey gently appeased his wife. He knew how useless it would be to argue: everybody was crazy. Now this thought was conclusively and definitely embedded in his mind. Concealing a yawn, he was trying to prove that Paiva was, in fact, very courteous, that her outer appearance was just a mannerism which might be explained by her varied life or perhaps by her modesty.

"She, modest? Only you could say that."

"Forget about her. . . . The reception was a success."

Madame Isabey agreed with him on this point. Everything had been very nice.

"Fould was very pleasant. But the Baron, there indeed is a charming gentleman. So gracious and handsome." Monsieur Isabey agreed reluctantly. He did not fancy the Senator.

"Yes, a very agreeable person."

"That is inadequate, 'agreeable.' He is simply charming. What a pity that he is a widower and much older than Henrietta. Why do you smile?" asked Madame Isabey, provoked. "I know how little you're interested in Henrietta. You're always thinking of your first family. I know perfectly that Henrietta and I mean nothing . . . Just so Eugene is well off."

Monsieur Isabey just as affectionately denied this; he loved her and Henrietta more than anyone else. Fould undoubtedly would find a husband for Henrietta. She was still very young.

Having calmed his wife, he kissed her on the forehead and went in the direction of his bedroom.

XVIII

❋❋❋

D URING the evening, in his bedroom, Monsieur Isabey had been sorting old papers, which had accumulated in great quantity. For this work, which had recently kept him busy, he had ordered a great number of folders, portfolios and indexes. Though Monsieur Isabey did not write much, he had, on his table, an abundance of variously colored pencils, splendidly cut pens, wax and containers with sand. Unsorted papers lay in the drawers of the desk. Monsieur Isabey placed the candle on the table, lighted another one, put on his glasses, sat down, and began cataloguing the papers. He took letters at random and tried, by the handwriting, to identify the sender; in the majority of cases he was successful. His visual memory was still exceptionally good but the handwriting brought back to him the face rather than the name He read some letters and without examination placed others in the proper folder. Those of no importance he threw into the fire: in the fireplace, near the table, embers still glowed. Monsieur Isabey knew that after his death these papers would be of interest

to no one, but he enjoyed the work. In a heap of
old letters Monsieur Isabey came across a card
with a mourning border. He looked at it reluctantly. The card was printed in German. "Yes, only
this evening we spoke of him. . . . But why did
we speak of him?" Monsieur Isabey could not
remember, and this vexed him. "Yes. What can one
do? My memory is failing. It seems I remember
my German a little. 'Constantina Domenica, Princess Razumovsky, born Countess von Thurhein,
Lady of the Star and Cross Order, begs to communicate . . .' Communicate what . . . 'word of
the death, tragic for her, of her deeply loved and
revered husband, His Royal Highness, Andreas,
Prince Razumovsky . . .' Yes. He was a wonderful
man. 'Knight of the Imperial . . .' This is about his
decorations. Yes, here are the decorations. 'To
Schwertberg in Austria, for interment in the family
vault . . .'" Monsieur Isabey read slowly guess-
ing rather than understanding the meaning of the
German words. "He was converted to the Catholic
faith before his death. His wife forced him to it
and also her sister, that canoness," thought Monsieur Isabey, disapprovingly: he was a Catholic
but maintained that everyone should die in the
faith in which he was born. "However, he
was always a Western man. It must have been
very hard for him. Why don't people leave one an-

other alone?" Monsieur Isabey was deliberating
into which folder to put the announcement, but
couldn't decide: he had not prepared a folder for
obituary notes. He sighed and threw the card into
the fireplace. The embers did not devour it at
once. In about a minute the flame caught at its
corner, the card flared up and the curled black ash
fell to the embers.

Monsieur Isabey worked until midnight, consulted the clock, stretched and with an effort
pulled himself up, bracing his hands against the
table, then caught his breath, removed the candles
and walked toward the tall chair against the wall.
He put the candles, which trembled in his hands,
on another table and made himself as comfortable
as possible for the night; cleaned his glasses and
reached for a thick book. Monsieur Isabey slept
very little, in snatches, at times not lasting more
than five or ten minutes. He usually read old jour-
nals with large type. He had complete. bound
volumes of them. Here were stories about what
had happened in the world during the past hundred years—Monsieur Isabey remembered nearly
all of it—biographies of famous people, Monsieur
Isabey had known nearly all of them.

He read, adding to the stories what he remembered, at times adding things from his imagina-
tion. His fantasy, as always, was very rich. When

he fell asleep he dreamed of the people who had
been the subject of his guests' conversation during
the previous evening. When he awoke he shuddered as the candlelight struck his eye, fixed his
glasses, with an effort picked up the fallen book,
and read again—or thought. He thought of how
beautiful life is, of how people do not appreciate it, of how little beauty they see in it and how
they poison it for themselves and, especially, for
others.